Praise for Sweet Tea and Jesus Shoes

"A sweeter, smoother-edged American South beckons from the pages...[of] a collection [that] conjures up the comfortable if ornery charms of a legendary culture."
—*Publishers Weekly*

"Storytelling is back with all its southern habits and charms. The stories are so good you'll be hungry for more."
—Liz Carpenter, acclaimed author and former press secretary for Lady Byrd Johnson

"Miss Julia would feel right at home on the front porches and in the living rooms and kitchens where these delightful stories originated."
—Ann B. Ross, author of *Miss Julia Speaks Her Mind*

"A brilliant compilation of southern women's stories in the tradition of Anne Rivers Siddons."
—Harriet Klausner, *Midwest Book Review*

"This book is rich in storytelling and makes me long for those days as a child listening to the stories of the past."
—Barbara Dooley, author, radio talk show host, and wife of University of Georgia Athletic Director, Vince Dooley.

"Sweet Tea and Jesus Shoes is a feast for any reader."
—Lisa Knighton, editor, *Georgia Women Speak*.

Praise for the authors of Sweet Tea and Jesus Shoes

"A major talent of the genre."
—Publishers Weekly

"Densely imagined...brilliant."
—Kirkus Reviews

"Mesmerizing...refreshing and compelling."
—Library Journal

"A story teller of distinction."
—BookPage

"Funny, suspenseful, and swift moving."
—Library Journal

"This talented newcomer...knows how to keep a tale moving."
—Kirkus Reviews

More Sweet Tea

BELLE BOOKS
Smyrna, GA

More Sweet Tea

Fly By Night *by Sarah Addison Allen*
Hair Today, Gone Tomorrow *by Maureen Hardegree*
The Fan Dancer *by Bert Goolsby*
The Healing Touch *by Susan Alvis*
The Hope Quilt *by Susan Goggins*
The Sun, the Moon, and a Box Of Divinity *by Clara Wimberly*
Dirty Harry, the Mule *by Mike Roberts*
Mommy Darlin *by Debra Dixon*
The Vinegar Files *by Lynda Holmes*
A Family Treasure *by Susan Sipal*
A Sunday Dress *by Betty Cordell*
Barbie's Elopement *by Sandra Chastain*
Drag Racer Arrested on Horseback *by Virginia Ellis*
The Mermaid of Cow Pie Spring *by Deborah Smith*

ISBN 0-9673035-9-1

Published by:

BelleBooks, Inc.
P.O. Box 67, Smyrna, Ga 30081

We at BelleBooks enjoy hearing from readers.
You can contact us at the address above or at BelleBooks@BelleBooks.com

Visit our website: www.BelleBooks.com

First Edition April 2005

10 9 8 7 6 5 4 3 2 1

Cover photograph: Gin Ellis
Cover design: Martha Shields
Interior design: John Cole
Copy Edit: Eric and Victoria Griffin

Table Of Contents

Fly By Night

by Sarah Addison Allen

True love is like ghosts, which everybody talks about and few have seen.
—Francois de La Rochfoucauld

I watched my house from the second-story bedroom at Great Aunt Sophie's. I could see that the lights were on in my living room. A shadow passed by the windows there, and the curtains moved like fingertips had brushed them.

My mom was slowly walking around our house next door, in and out of each room, like she was looking for someone. The kitchen light went on once, then flicked back off.

"Louise!" Great Aunt Sophie called from the next room, and my elbows jerked off the windowsill where I was kneeling. "Go to sleep."

There was no door, just a doorway, between Great Aunt Sophie's bedroom and the one I was sleeping in that night. As I knelt at the open window, pretending I was in bed asleep, I could hear her turning the pages of her book, the low mumble of the radio station out of Asheville that still played big band music, and sometimes I even heard the rattle of ice cubes as she poured iced tea into a hard plastic cup from the thermos she brought up from the kitchen. They had the easy, sleepy echo of sounds repeated night after night. Great Aunt Sophie herself was like that. She was worn in the best possible way, like the way your oldest shoes fit, the shoes that wouldn't slip when you ran on dewy grass and gave you traction when climbing hickory trees.

I ignored Great Aunt Sophie with the hope that she was just checking to see if I was asleep. If I didn't say anything, she would surely believe that I was. I turned back to the window I was kneeling in front of and continued to watch my house. The night outside was the thick black of a new moon and lightning bugs ticked away in backyards as far as I could see. My bedroom next door was dark, but suddenly light spilled faintly into the room, as if the switch in the bedroom across the hall from mine had been turned on. The light covered my doorway and outlined the toy horses I'd placed on my windowsill that very morning.

"Louise," Great Aunt Sophie called. "Don't make me say it again."

I should have known that she knew. She knew everything. She knew things nobody else knew.

I got up and walked to the doorway separating the two bedrooms. Her room had side-by-side twin beds, both covered with pink, quilted polyester bedspreads. She slept in the one on the left, farthest from the door and nearest to the open window. The bedroom I was staying in had one full bed with a knotty pine headboard pushed against the wall. The mattress was an old featherbed, and it felt a lot like sleeping on a nest of pine needles. I knew this because I fell out of a pine tree once and landed in a pile of needles, breath gone, thinking I was dead, and I looked up to see Great Aunt Sophie in her straw hat. I thought that was a horrible way to go, lying in resiny needles with Great Aunt Sophie's frown the last thing I would see. She told me to go home because she was in no mood for my antics and she hadn't raked that pile of pine needles just for me to jump in. I thought she had no respect for the dying, so I went home to tell my mother, who didn't believe me because I was breathing again.

Great Aunt Sophie and her husband Harry used to sleep in the featherbed room, but Great Aunt Sophie moved into the room with the pink twin beds after Harry died. My mom told my dad this once, as if trying to explain away some of Great Aunt Sophie's peculiarities. I didn't like the thought of sleeping in the featherbed room. I had never met my great-uncle and I didn't know if it was possible to be haunted by someone you had never known, but I didn't want to risk it.

"Go to sleep," Great Aunt Sophie said, laying her open book page-down on her chest and folding her fingers over it tightly, hiding the picture on the cover.

"It won't come. I tried."

"Then get yourself into bed. Sleep can't come into your head if you're sitting up at that window."

I walked into her room. There were places in Great Aunt Sophie's house where certain scents pooled. As you walked in the front door, you smelled Blue Grass perfume right away. Great Aunt Sophie kept the spritzer in a table drawer beside the door and always sprayed her gloves once before going to church. Then there was that place on her staircase, about three steps up, that for no reason smelled like lavender, as if just moments before a beautiful lady had walked up the stairs ahead of you. And in the twin-bed room, it smelled of yellowy paperback romance novels and Rosemilk lotion, the kind they advertised during *The Lawrence Welk Show.*

I sat on the edge of the twin bed next to hers. She had taken the thin pink bedspread off her bed and folded it neatly at the bottom of the bed I was sitting on. She was on top of her sheets in deference to the cloying summertime heat, and her sunbrown bare feet were crossed at the ankles. She had reddish-orange polish on her toenails and caked around her cuticles and skin, like she'd had trouble aiming the brush. For as long as I knew her, she'd always painted her nails this way, and I had no choice but to believe she did it on purpose.

"Mom can't sleep, either. I was watching her. She's walking around the house."

"It's understandable, Louise. Let her walk and tire herself out. Then she'll sleep. You'll see her tomorrow," she said, as if tomorrow weren't so far away.

Great Aunt Sophie was as practical as a pin. She intimidated me sometimes with her perfect rightness. She never had any children. I never asked why, but sometimes I thought it was because she didn't like kids. She didn't have much patience with me. Her husband, Harry, died when she was in her forties, and she never remarried. My dad had once said he could never imagine Great Aunt Sophie married. My mom told him that there were certain hurts that Sophie chose not to show, but that didn't mean they weren't there.

"Do you ever miss Harry?" I asked, just to keep her talking so I could stay longer in her room.

Great Aunt Sophie looked straight ahead, not at me, as if seeing long ago things I couldn't see, maybe even the ghost in the next room. "Of course I do."

"After so long?"

"Yes," she said shortly, closing up her secrets. "You shouldn't be asking me these questions. You should be asleep."

"I miss my dad," I finally said. I had been afraid to say it all day, afraid that I was the only one.

Great Aunt Sophie paused, then nodded, just once. "I know you do."

I was surprised. Mom and Great Aunt Sophie had acted so normally that day. They smiled and accepted condolences as easily as they would have accepted a compliment, graciously and without fuss. I didn't understand. I didn't feel normal. It hadn't been a normal day for me.

"Do you miss him, too?" I asked, because Great Aunt Sophie and my dad didn't get along and I was afraid that she was glad now that he was gone. They were friendly enough, I suppose. But Great Aunt Sophie couldn't put the fear of God in him with just a look like she could with most people, and I think that annoyed her.

"Your daddy was a dreamer. He could dance, and that was in his favor." She slanted her eyes my way. "Never marry a man who can't dance, Louise."

Knowing how to dance was important to Great Aunt Sophie. Sometimes, when she took her bicycle out of the garage, she would do a little two-step with it if she was in a good mood. She loved her bicycle. I remember seeing her once, dressed in her Sunday-go-to-meeting finest, pedaling past our house on her way to church. Then I remember seeing the back of her dress fly up, right in front of old Harvey Williams, who had opted to walk to church that morning with his wife Annie because he was having one of his good days. From then until the day he died, he referred to that incident as his Sunday morning revelation. When my mom wanted to vex Great Aunt Sophie, she would bring this up.

I scratched at a circle of poison ivy on my leg, just above my knee. It had been hard to sit still at the funeral service that morning and not scratch. I had tried to think of everything I could remember about the last time I saw my dad, to take my mind off the itch. I was in my nightgown in the kitchen, waiting for my Lucky Charms. He had his steel lunch box. He checked the refrigerator again to see if he had forgotten his thermos of orange juice. I could remember things he usually said: Goodbye. I love you. Where's my orange juice? But I couldn't remember if he said those things that morning or, if he did, in what order.

"Louise, stop scratching that, or it will never get better," Great Aunt Sophie told me.

I did as she said. "I want to be home."

"Your mama needs to be alone tonight. You're a yard away. It's silly to miss a person who's only a yard away."

I opened my mouth and thought about that for a minute, knowing Great Aunt Sophie didn't suffer talking off the top of your head. "But it's okay to miss the people far off, right?"

Great Aunt Sophie nodded twice. "That's when you should miss them."

I'd never seen Great Aunt Sophie show an emotion stronger than indignation, and that one was her favorite. But I knew she loved me, just as I knew she loved my mom. She raised my mom from the time my mom was ten, when her mother died. My grandmother was Great Aunt Sophie's sister and she married a "no-good sailor man" that Great Aunt Sophie didn't like so much she never even said his name. He was still living, somewhere. No one ever mentioned where.

Sometimes it seemed like she was still raising my mom. She participated actively in everything my mom did, except for when she married my dad. Defiantly, they went to South Carolina and eloped. My dad used to say it took the summer Mom discovered she was pregnant with me for Great Aunt Sophie to finally give her blessing. That was a grand summer, he'd said. Warm weather and the promise of only good things to come.

It surprised me that Great Aunt Sophie wasn't hovering around Mom now, giving her a break from thinking, tonight of all nights. But Great Aunt Sophie had talked to my mom only once since we got home, and that was to say goodnight. She didn't even offer food. Great Aunt Sophie *always* offered food. Everyone knew that. In times of distress she could whip up green bean casseroles, broccoli cornbread, and peanut butter pies, then be at the doorstep of the bereaved before most folks in the factory town of Clementine, North Carolina, even knew there had been a tragedy.

I didn't know whose idea it was for me to stay with Great Aunt Sophie that night. If I had been sure Mom was responsible, I might have been able to talk her out of it. But if it had been Great Aunt Sophie's idea, I knew arguing with her would be like throwing a stone up to try to hurt the sky. She was that vast, that unshakable. She thundered only when she wanted to. So I didn't say a thing as Sophie took a pair of pajamas out of my dresser and took my hand to lead me across our yard into hers after we all got home that afternoon.

She gave me cream of tomato soup, which she had made from her own tomatoes, and then she melted some shredded cheddar cheese on saltine crackers in the oven. While I ate at her kitchen table, which was covered with a printed oilcloth, she took her garden shears and went outside. That night I discovered that she'd picked some Shasta daises and put them in a vase in the featherbed room for me.

I tried to scoot slowly, invisibly, to the top of the twin bed, so Great Aunt Sophie wouldn't see what I was doing and order me back to the ghost room. "Why doesn't everybody go to heaven, Aunt Sophie?" I asked as I put my head on the pillow.

"God decides that, not me," she said, though I knew she had her own ideas on the subject.

I stared at the textured ceiling. "Do you think my dad's in heaven?"

My dad knew of heaven. He didn't go to church, but I think he understood the idea.

The winter before, on a cold, still Appalachian night in December, he had come in from somewhere, I don't remember where, and he was smiling. He smelled like the cold and cigarette smoke when he picked me up and carried me outside without even giving me time to put on my coat. My mom only smiled at him the way she always did, as if she loved him so much she couldn't speak.

The snow had hushed the neighborhood. It was so quiet that each step he took in the hard snow sounded like the pop of a paper bag full of air. Once we were in the front yard, he put me down, then pointed up. I followed his finger to the millions of bright stars overhead. There were so many of them it looked like there was no night, just stars, packed like an audience trying to get a better view of us.

"Look at that, Louise," he said in awe. "God, will you look at that. There you go."

There you go.

"Is that where he went?"

Great Aunt Sophie was silent for a good many moments. She reached over and took a bookmark off the table to her right. She marked the place in her book and set it aside. "I've pondered this now," she finally said. "And I believe your daddy's in heaven. Dreaming and dancing are heavenly things. Your daddy would fit right in."

"Your Harry's in heaven, I guess," I said.

"Yes, he is." She took a quick, deep, decision-making breath. "Do you want to know why I took that door away, Louise?" She pointed to the doorway separating the rooms. "It's because I can lie here and look into that room and see where he lived. My memories are in there, but my life is in here. That's the way it is, Louise. You can look at them, but you can't live them."

"I want to be home." I tried to keep my voice straight so Great Aunt Sophie wouldn't know I was crying. She didn't like for people to cry. It made her fidget. She all but left the room when Lorelei Horton tearfully told the Sunday school committee that her son was finally coming home from Vietnam.

I woke up just after two in the morning, and static was coming from Great Aunt Sophie's clock radio. The big band station out of Asheville signed off at two and resumed broadcasting at six. I was still in the bed next to Great Aunt Sophie's. She had covered me with the scratchy bedspread. I looked over to her and saw that she was asleep, breathing through her mouth. The static didn't seem to bother her.

I got out of bed, half-asleep, and went to the featherbed ghost room, my need to make sure my house was still there greater than my fear of being haunted. I knelt at the window again and stared at my house. Every single light was on now, even the front and back porch lights. It looked like the sun had fallen into the house and was shining out of every opening the hot yellow light could find. Even the basement light was on. I could see the shine crawling out of the one window in the bricks at the bottom of the house. That was my dad's wonder room. He made stuff there, fixed stuff, too. He fixed Great Aunt Sophie's coffee percolator once, which I thought was very nice of him.

I rested my chin in my hands. The static from the radio was becoming familiar now and it was lulling me back to sleep. But that's when I noticed something on the roof of my house. I lifted my head and stared hard, trying to make out what it was.

The figure moved from between the dormer windows at the front of the house, to the edge of the back of the house. She wore a white nightgown I could see in the darkness. She sort of danced around the rooftop for a while, like she was testing her balance. I didn't understand her presence on my rooftop. Before tonight, I'd never had the perspective of looking out over my house. I wondered if she had visited before, or if tonight was special.

The lights from the house illuminated her figure like stage lights. She went to the edge of the roof and held her arms out wide like she was going to fly.

I remember thinking, *She can do it. She can fly.*

Then I heard a sound over the static, like a voice rising above applause. The angel standing on my roof was crying. It was the unhappiest sound I'd ever heard. The hurt in it pricked my skin like someone had pinched me, and tears came to my eyes.

She doesn't want to fly.

Then she lifted her hands up to the sky as if asking for help from God. She put her hands on top of her head and tucked her chin to her chest. Was she praying?

God, help me not fly.

I heard some movement in the next room, like maybe Great Aunt Sophie had gotten out of bed and gone to her window. Then I think maybe she said, "Good Lord in heaven, no."

I closed my eyes and felt the warmth from the light from my house. I hoped the angel would stay, that she wouldn't fly away since the thought was agonizing her so. I remember hearing Great Aunt Sophie saying softly, over and over, "Don't do it, don't do it, don't do it."

But I couldn't help it. I had to go to sleep.

When I woke up again, it was morning. The air was wet with the scent of cut grass and gasoline. Someone was mowing somewhere in the neighborhood. I was lying on the floor, below the window, and Great Aunt Sophie's pink polyester bedspread was again covering me. I sat up and looked around. I could hear voices coming from outside, so I crawled to the window and looked out. Great Aunt Sophie was down in her rose garden, and my mom was hanging her favorite green-and-white striped bed sheets on the clothesline in our backyard. They were talking to each other, calling back and forth like they did almost every sunny day when there was outdoor work to be done.

"Mom!" I yelled.

Both she and Great Aunt Sophie turned at the sound of my voice. Mom smiled up at me. "Come over here and give me a hug, sweetie girl," she called.

And I was out of the house in nothing flat.

I ran right past Great Aunt Sophie and over to my mother. As I hugged her, I grabbed her shirt tight in my fists as if she would fly away if I let go, as if I'd caught her just in time. She bent down and kissed the top of my head. She was fine, the way all Southern ladies were fine, as if there were no hurts great enough to break them. But I knew there were, and I held her tighter.

Great Aunt Sophie watched us, her hand shielding her eyes from the sun. She stood there for a long time. Finally, she lowered her hand and picked up her basket of roses. She walked back to her house and her ghost there, and Mom and I held hands and walked slowly together to our house to greet ours.

Hair Today, Gone Tomorrow

by Maureen Hardegree

It's hard for me to get used to these changing times. I can remember when the air was clean and sex was dirty.
—George Burns

I've lived a good life, and I've seen a lot of change in the eighty-seven years I've been in this world. Some changes have been first rate, like the cordless phone and the paper sack. I bet you don't know too many women who can remember when the paper sack was invented. But I have to tell you, not all change is good.

Take hairdressers, for example. I can guarantee losing a hairdresser is one of the worst things that can happen to a woman, worse even than hot flashes. I know this for a fact. I've lost several to retirement, one to a divorce, and two to arthritis. But I hadn't ever lost one to the cemetery until last week.

And if you don't think that's bad, then maybe you can tell me how the H-E-double-L a town-full of old women are supposed to get their hair done for a funeral when the only hairdresser in town who knows how to fix hair right is the one they're going to see buried. It's what you might call a real predicament.

That's what I was trying to figure out last week at breakfast right after Geneva called to inform me of the blow fate had dealt to the old women of Mayburn.

The smell of sausage and biscuits hung in the air as I took my first bite. I nearly choked when my phone rang. I checked the clock on the wall, then my wristwatch with the big numbers my grandson gave me because my eyesight's so poor these days. It wasn't but ten after eight. Who could be calling me so early in the morning? I hadn't even had time to read the obituaries yet.

"I'm coming, I'm coming," I said to the phone, annoyed because everyone knows there's nothing worse than a cold biscuit. I went to the bedroom off my kitchen. That was where my cordless phone was sleeping in its cradle.

"Hello?" I said, hoping it wasn't one of those salespeople. My grandson put me on the national "don't call me" list, so it should be someone I knew.

"Lucille, it's Geneva. I've got terrible news." My across-the-street neighbor's voice crackled over the phone. For Geneva, terrible news could be weevils in her cold cereal, so I didn't get all excited.

I walked over to the front room and peeked out my dusty Venetian blinds. Geneva was standing by her picture window and looking at my house. She had every light in that building lit, wasting money. Now me, I like to keep my light bill low.

"What kind of terrible news?" I shouted.

"Have you read the obituaries yet?"

"No."

"Then go do it, right now."

My heart raced in my chest, and my head got a little swimmy, so I walked back to the kitchen table and sat down. One thing I don't do is go all to pieces, but I had a head cold today and got a little teary-eyed. I flipped to the page of the *Mayburn Times* listing all the deaths.

The first one was a full-blown article about a teenager driving too fast, who killed himself smacking into a tree. "Now that's a downright shame," I said. "That boy's family must be a mess about now. It's a terrible thing when your kids go before you do." I knew the truth of what I said because I'd lived it.

The family's last name wasn't familiar. He must not have grown up around these parts—sounded kind of Yankee, if you asked me. And they lived in one of those new subdivisions popping up all over town.

"No, no," Geneva fussed. "Look at the last one."

"Don't get your drawers in a wad. I'm getting there." My eyes scanned down, and I saw what had her so upset. Pearl Malcolm was dead.

"That can't be," I said, more to myself than to Geneva. I'd seen Pearl in the market the other day, and I should've told her she looked like she was ailing, but I hadn't because it just wouldn't have been polite. We'd talked about me needing a permanent.

She'd told me to come over around eight o'clock Saturday morning, her first appointment of the day. Looked like I wouldn't be going now.

"It's true enough." Geneva harrumphed. "The paper don't say it, but Pearl knew something was wrong. Lida was having her hair fixed, and she could tell Pearl was feeling puny. Lida called Pearl's daughter, Mary Clare, the one who works at that fancy hairdresser in the strip mall . . ."

You could say Mary Clare had followed in her mama's footsteps if not scissor hands.

"Well, Mary Clare was trying to get Pearl to leave and go to the 'mergency room in Monroe," Geneva said, and took a breath, "but Pearl wouldn't listen. She told Mary Clare she wasn't leaving until everybody's appointment was taken care of."

"Says here she had a heart attack." Of course, it didn't say right out that she had a heart attack. That wasn't done. But it did say she "died suddenly," and we all knew what that meant. If it had said she died after a prolonged illness, we'd have known it was cancer. And if it said someone died "unexpectedly," well, we'd pray for the family. "Unexpectedly" meant suicide.

"Lordy, lordy, that's not the half of it. Lida told Essie Mae Walton that once Pearl was ready to go to the hospital, she caught sight of herself in the mirror. She started trimming her bangs. I guess she was worried about them doctors seeing her hair shaggy, her being a hairdresser and all. About half-way through cutting them, she fell out."

"She dropped dead right there?"

"Don't you know it. The worst part is that she's got a chunk of hair missing at the center of her forehead, looks just like a kindergartener who got hold of her first pair of scissors. I don't know who Mr. Bowden's gonna get to fix her for the viewin'."

I didn't know who was going to fix my hair, either. Then I felt badly for thinking it.

"That's terrible," I agreed. "Just plain terrible."

"Don't you know it," Geneva said. "And I'd like to know who's gonna do our hair for the viewin' and the funeral? I ain't goin' to that hoity-toity place where Mary Clare works. I hear there's a man there. Calls hisself a *stylist*."

"I don't mean to be ugly, but you shouldn't be worrying about your hair at a time like this, Geneva." Good thing she didn't have the gift of reading minds.

Pearl, bless her heart, had been a good woman, and I'd miss her. You could say we were friends of sorts. Women are close to their hairdressers; it's a fact of life. We tell hairdressers some stuff we don't even tell our families. Hairdressers know all about your kids, and your grandkids, and if you've lived as long as me, even your great-grandkids.

She had a small beauty parlor in a converted garage. She always did let me have the first appointment of the day because I didn't like to wait. It made me nervous. Her poodle Jezebel was always wanting to sit in my lap, and I'd learned to tolerate it. Never did understand treating dogs like babies, but then there were a lot of things in this world I didn't understand, like why people were against the truckers. Trucks were how we got our food. People forgot that.

I hung up with Geneva, and I hated to admit it, but when I set the phone back in its cradle, I took a look at my hair in the mirror. It was a flat-out mess. I'd been due for a perm for over a month, but I'd put it off.

I checked my calendar and right smack dab on Saturday was my appointment to have my perm. I couldn't show up to the viewing with my hair all flat; it wasn't respectful—especially when the person who was dead made her living fixing people's hair. I was going to have to figure out something fast, as would the rest of the town's over-seventy crowd.

What in the world was Geneva going to do? Pearl was the only hairdresser in three counties who knew what a finger wave was, much less how to do one.

Maybe a hat would work. I knew I must have some from years ago. I don't throw much away. You never know when you might need it.

I went to my wardrobe and looked in the drawers. The only things I saw were lots of underwear that were too big since I started falling off. I didn't eat much these days. And the dress, slip, and nylons I'm going to wear to *my* funeral were in the second drawer I checked. I showed them to my grandson's wife the last time she visited, so she'd know where everything was, and she agreed my outfit was right pretty.

Suffice to say, I couldn't find one of my old hats to save my life. I must have put them up in the attic, and I wasn't going up there. I like to have killed myself tottering on the ladder last time I tried, and my grandson made me promise not to do it anymore.

I wasn't supposed to rake leaves from the hateful tree out back, either, but I did it anyway. I figured minding about the attic was good enough to suit him.

I realized I was going to have to buy a hat to cover up my hair, and that would mean a trip to the mall with my sister Carolyn, who I'd raised like she was my own.

That was one of those changes that was nowhere as good as a paper sack—shopping malls. The only stores we got left in what people in Atlanta called our "quaint" town were restaurants and antique stores, and not one of them had a hat I could wear to Pearl's viewing.

While Carolyn tried to find a parking space near one of the entrances, I counted my cash. I don't buy a thing on credit. If you want something, you save up for it.

Two hundred dollars. Plenty, and then some. I removed a twenty and secured my wad of bills with a rubber band and slipped it back into the special zippered compartment of my pocket book. You never know when you might have an emergency like a flat tire and need some cash money to have it fixed. I believe in being prepared.

Carolyn parked the car as close to the Rich's entrance as she could get. I know about how Macy's bought them, but I refuse to call the store anything else. Anyway, the entrance looked to be about a mile away from where she parked.

Once we got inside the store, Carolyn walked me over to some hats. They were all sports caps like the kind my grandson likes to wear. I supposed I could wear a Braves cap since Pearl was such a fan. She'd always had the game on during baseball season.

A nice man pointed us to where the ladies' hats were, on the other side of the brightly lit center of the store where they sell all that perfume, jewelry, and make-up.

I'd read about fraternity boys and midshipmen having to run the gauntlet when being hazed, and I felt like I was right there with them as Carolyn and I tried to cross that slippery marble floor and avoid the pretty women in chiffon scarves shoving perfume-squirted cards into our hands. Girls in white doctor coats offered to give us makeovers.

"I'm just here to buy a hat," I said and placed the perfume cards on a nearby glass counter; they were stopping up my head.

When we made it to the ladies' hats section, wouldn't you know, I couldn't find but one black hat among all they had for sale.

Carolyn made me try it on. "Let me see, dahlin'." She clapped her hands together. "Now don't you look pretty."

I stared in the mirror. "What I look like is ridiculous. No one wants to see an old, pasty-faced woman in wide-brimmed black hat that belongs on some movie starlet from the 1940's."

A very nice saleslady, who favored the Stanton family, came over to help us.

"Are you related to the Stantons?" I asked.

She frowned slightly as she searched the hat stands for something that would work for a funeral. "I don't know. "

"Who's your mama's people?" I asked.

"Her last name was Inman before she married my daddy. Betty Inman."

"Betty Inman?" I pondered that name for a minute. "Is she the younger sister of Margaret Inman?"

The saleslady blinked. "How did you know?"

"All right now, my mind is going back. Your mama's grandmother was a Stanton. She went to the music school with my mama."

The saleslady didn't seem impressed, but then she pulled out a straw hat with a wide black ribbon around the crown. "Straw is very *in* this spring," she said.

"It won't go with my black pant suit," I said.

Now pants for women was a change I had taken to readily. If I didn't have to show my chubby legs in a pair of nylons, I wasn't going to.

But the salesgirl, who looked like a Stanton if I ever did see one, wanted me to try on the silly hat anyway. And Carolyn wanted to see me in it as well. I knew it was a bad idea, but I put it on purely out of politeness.

I looked like Bette Davis in that Baby Jane movie.

"No, thank you," I said.

"But, honey, what're you gonna do?" Carolyn asked. "The viewing is less than twenty-four hours away."

"Well, I'm sure as H-E-double-L not gonna wear this damn hat," I said.

The next morning, the morning of the viewing I might add, Carolyn carted me off to that strip mall hairdresser's shop where Pearl's daughter Mary Clare worked. A sign in the window said "Walk-ins Welcome."

I saw some of the women coming out and told Carolyn I thought this was a bad idea. I pointed at the one whose hair was sticking out every which way, like she'd just rolled out of bed and stuck her finger in the light socket. The woman following her had hair straight as a board and parted down the middle.

Women today don't know how to fix their hair. The styles are just plain ugly.

"Now, you're going in, Lucille. Everything's gonna be all right, doll, you'll see."

A big sign hanging down from the ceiling tiles above the cash register listed prices for everything but what I wanted. Waxing, pedicures, manicures, massages. Where were the words *wash and set*?

"It's too expensive," I whispered to Carolyn.

"Hush," she said. "What would Pearl think?"

"How can I help you?" asked a girl with short, spiky, bleached-blond hair.

I didn't answer at first because there was a piece of something hanging under her lip. It winked in the light like an earring. Now that's a change I'll never understand. Why in the world do young people want to stick earrings in places they don't belong? If God had meant for us to have holes all over our bodies, he would've made us that way.

"Ma'am," she said, and the earring bobbed.

"I need to get my hair done."

"So a cut and blow dry?"

"I don't want no blow dry, that's what makes women's hair look so bad today." I craned my neck to see past the front counter. "Haven't you got any real hairdryers?"

Carolyn stepped up to the counter. "Lucille just wants her hair fixed, dahlin'. You know, maybe a little trim and set in curlers."

"Yes, ma'am. We'll fit her in as soon as we can. It'll be about fifteen minutes' wait before we have someone free."

"Their sign says walk-ins welcome," I mumbled under my breath. I don't like waiting; it makes me nervous. The viewing started at four o'clock. It was eleven, now.

I don't guess the girl heard me because right about then Mary Clare walked in. Her eyes were red from crying. She's a pretty woman, looks a lot like Reba McEntire.

Mary Clare's been divorced twice. And when she was over at her mama's, she was always suggesting her mama's customers update their look. She meant well, but old people don't want to update their look. They like their look just fine.

"Girl, what are you doing here?" a man shouted from the back of the salon.

"Ernest and I just got done with the funeral arrangements, and I gotta keep myself busy," Mary Clare said. "Besides, cuttin' hair makes me feel close to Mama."

Ernest was Mary Clare's brother. He was in the construction business.

She started boo-hooing, and I felt sorry for anyone sitting in Mary Clare's chair today. Didn't seem like she'd be able to do a good job.

When she went off to the back to find some tissue to blow her nose, I took a bottle of fancy shampoo from the display shelf. I focused my eyes on the price and nearly fell out myself. That glorified soap cost more than my monthly water bill.

After exactly twenty-nine minutes, the pierced girl called me back for my shampoo. Only that's not what she did. She started rubbing on my shoulders and my scalp. She told me it was a massage. I told her I wasn't paying extra for it, and she stopped.

I had a bit of a fright when I noticed this woman sitting in the hairdresser man's chair. He was painting strands of her hair purple and wrapping them in tin foil. The pieces stood up, and she looked like a silver foil dandelion.

My eyes must have widened because Carolyn whispered, "It's okay, doll. We won't let them do that to you."

I warned the shampoo girl that I had a tender scalp and was allergic to most everything. She didn't seem to be paying me much attention. She was singing to the dance music blaring over the loudspeaker.

Other than that oddly placed earring, she looked familiar. "What's your name?" I asked.

She glanced down at her nametag that said *Chloe*. "Huh?"

"Your last name, what is it?"

"Johnson."

"Johnson," I repeated as she helped me to an empty chair near the sink to wait my turn for a hairdresser. "I believe my son Eddie went to school with a Johnson. Did your daddy live over yonder near the hub?"

A white limousine drove up and captured everyone's attention before the girl could answer.

"Would you look at that," Carolyn said, more to herself than me.

A group of giggling young women came in.

"Here's the bride," Mary Clare said with a trembly smile, then she dropped the hand mirror she was using to check the back of her hair.

"Seven years bad luck," I said and shook my head. "She don't need that, considering she lost her mama."

"Miss Lucille," the pierced girl named Chloe said, "I'm afraid you're going to have to wait. We've got to get the wedding party ready. I was hoping to have you under the dryer before they got here, but they're early, and they have appointments."

She went off to sweep up the mess Mary Clare made.

Carolyn patted my hand. "It'll be all right. You have plenty of time, doll."

After many hugs, the bride was escorted to the sink next to me. She was right pretty, and I hoped she'd have her hair styled properly. I smiled at her, and she smiled back. Seemed like I'd seen a smile like hers before. Couldn't think of where, though.

"Congratulations," I said. "So this is your big day."

"Yes, ma'am. We're having our reception at Magnolia Manor."

Sounded to me like her family was putting on the dog, but

if that's how people wanted to waste their money. . . "Do you know I got married in nineteen and thirty for twenty-five dollars? Marry a sweet man, I always say. I hope your husband's sweet."

"Yes, ma'am." She smiled again, and a dimple showed in her left cheek, reminding me of someone I'd known in the past.

That crooked smile and dimple took my mind right back to the schoolhouse. Buford Hamby. "You aren't by chance related to a Buford Hamby, are you?"

"He's my great-grandfather."

"I knew it. I knew it. You got a smile just like him. We went to school together. We weren't sweethearts or nothin'. Truth is, he was sweet on the teacher. Do you know he locked the rest of us out of the schoolhouse one day? He was a bit older than me, but we was all in the same room back in then. He wanted to be alone with our teacher, so's he could court her."

The young bride smiled politely, then craned her neck to see one of her bridesmaids. "Yes, ma'am."

"I bet you didn't know that," I said. "I tell you what, I'm going to give you some of the best advice I know for a good marriage. Are you listening to me, now?"

The bride nodded. I had her undivided attention.

"Most men like a good dessert. You bake enough cakes and pies and your husband won't go to no kitchen but your own."

"I'll remember that," she said as they eased her back to wash her hair.

I was a mite worried they'd never get to me before the viewing, plus I was hungry. But I wasn't about to leave and lose my spot or let Mary Clare get a hold of my hair. One of the bridesmaids had a weepy Mary Clare working on her, and the results were . . . Let's just say I hadn't seen hair ratted that high since nineteen hundred and sixty-nine. The bridesmaid, who'd come in giggling, didn't look none too happy when Mary Clare then sprayed her hair with enough shellac that I coughed sitting twenty feet away.

I'm sure that's not what the young bridesmaid wanted but, bless her heart, I guess Mary Clare did it as some sort of tribute to her mama. Pearl would have been proud.

The hairdresser man noticed my discomfort and offered to do my hair. I took a good look at him. His hair was as long as a woman's and had bleached streaks in it. He'd either been to the beach recently or he'd gotten one of those fake tans from a can I read about. From what I'd seen, he'd been giving the women in his chair messed up hair all morning, and I wasn't going to let him update my look.

"I'll wait for one of the women to be through," I said, then leaned over to whisper to Carolyn who was sitting on the other side of me. "If I'd wanted a man to fix my hair, I'd have gone to a barber shop."

Carolyn said she'd let him do hers. I think my whispering was too loud, and I embarrassed her.

A woman in pale yellow sweatpants motioned for me to come over to her chair. Carolyn helped me walk over—in case I got swimmy-headed.

In the middle of trimming my hair, this lady got a call on her cell phone. She just up and left me sitting in her chair, me with my hair halfway trimmed. I looked at the clock on the wall, and then my wristwatch. I'd already been here two hours.

"Now, sis," Carolyn said, "we've got plenty of time. I'm sure it was an emergency."

The emergency turned out to be some grandchild wanting a happy meal. While I waited, I watched in horror as Mary Clare fouled up another bridesmaid's hair. Not knowing any better, the girl asked Mary Clare to trim her bangs. Before I could whistle Dixie, the girl was nearly bald. I'd never seen a woman's hair as short except possibly some of the women patients at the radiation clinic where I went for treatments after my lumpectomy.

All I wanted to do at this point was leave, but my hair looked worse than when I came in. I couldn't go to the viewing looking like I did with one side of my head cut. I wasn't fit to be seen.

Mary Clare finished with her half of the bridal party and told me she'd take me since the happy meal lady hadn't returned yet. As a former customer of her mama's, I was right grateful, because I knew she knew how to roll an old woman's hair. Yet I was a wee bit scared after seeing the lady before me scalped.

"I believe in holding up my commitments," Mary Clare said. "Mama taught me that."

She sniffed and lifted her scissors. Before she started snipping off big hanks of my hair, I told her, "That's okay, Mary Clare. You just take yourself a break. I'm waitin' on the man."

The man hairdresser, who wanted to be called a stylist and who smelled right nice, helped me over to what he called his station. "So I'm the lesser of two evils, Miss Lucille?"

I ignored his comment and told him how I liked my hair done.

He trimmed it too short and picked out the wrong-sized rollers.

I told him as much. "Listen," I said, "Those aren't the right rollers. Pearl always used the pink ones."

Mary Clare, who'd come back from her break, started crying again.

The man hairdresser finished rolling my hair with the wrong-sized rollers. But I'll give him one thing, he was fast.

Unfortunately, because he didn't mind me, when I got out from under the dryer, my hair looked like Pearl's poodle's coat, and that made Mary Clare cry all the more. Apparently, Jezebel ran away that morning when they let her out of the house to go tee-tee.

I'd never been so worn out by something in all my born days—not even walking on a broken hip. And I'd thought going to the mall was bad. My hairdresser man asked me if I wanted to schedule another appointment in six weeks.

"And just what in the H-E-double-L do you think you can do to it then? I won't have any hair left."

He laughed and handed me his business card anyway.

I decided maybe he wasn't so bad, but the whole day had me in such a state that I forgot to give him his dollar tip.

Mary Clare's latest man friend was holding her up at the viewing. Geneva told me his name was Emory, like the university, and that he worked for the post office over in Monroe. He made a good living; maybe he was just what Mary Clare needed to finally settle down.

I hoped she'd been paying attention to my advice to that young bride about making dessert. Cakes and pies definitely were the shortest path to a man's heart. Maybe even a hairdresser's if that man was a *stylist*.

I pondered for a minute and looked at all the old women around me. Most were wearing black hats. Mrs. Duval, whose hair had always been a lovely shade of blue when Pearl gave it a rinse, was now an unnatural lavender purple color. The hair on the back of Geneva's head was as flat as a pancake.

All in all, I decided that my stylist at the strip mall wasn't so bad. He was fast, too. You had to respect a man who could roll hair faster than a woman.

I went up to the casket and looked at how nicely Mr. Bowden had Pearl laid out. Her hair was absolutely beautiful, that shade of honey blonde she liked—she'd been pretending she was a true blonde since nineteen hundred and seventy-two when she graduated from beauty school. You couldn't even tell there was a chunk missing from her bangs. I wondered if whoever they'd found to do her hair had used one of those weaves I'd read about.

I made my way over to Mary Clare and patted her hand. "Your mama looks just beautiful."

"Yeah," she agreed. "Ronnie did a great job."

"Ronnie who?" I said.

"Ronnie McKibbens."

I moved along and made my condolences to Mary Clare's brother Ernest, then pulled the business card out of my handbag and read the name. Ronnie McKibbens.

Sure enough, the hairdresser man who did my hair did Pearl's hair, too.

I wondered if he was related to the McKibbens who lived over in the next county. I bet not one of Ronnie's customers made him homemade pies or cakes or even banana pudding. The only customers I'd seen were under thirty, and young women today don't know much about cooking. I could probably train him to do my hair the way I liked. I could definitely win his heart with my award-winning fried pies. And with him being so young, I surely wouldn't outlive him and have to go through this whole mess again.

Like I said earlier, change is difficult. But you have to be open to change—even if you don't like it and especially when it involves hairdressers. Anyone who tells you different, doesn't know what in the H-E-double-L he's talking about.

The Fan Dancer

by Bert Goolsby

My mother had a great deal of trouble with me,
but I think she enjoyed it.
—Mark Twain

When God calls me home, I imagine it will be somewhat akin to the time the principal summoned me to his office. The call will come without warning and it will scare the pure and tee devil out of me—which is not a bad thing when you think about it.

Anyway, one Friday afternoon, while I sat in Miss Lillian Snipe's twelfth-grade government class bored slap out of my mind, an announcement came over the classroom loudspeaker. A feminine voice stated that Mr. Goodhart wanted to see me in his office immediately. Mr. Goodhart served as the high school principal—a nice man, but a person to avoid, especially in his office.

Everyone in class turned and looked toward me, a question registered on each one's face. Like them, I didn't know what I had done or, more accurately, been caught doing.

Miss Snipe scowled at me as I got up from my back-row desk and slipped up the aisle toward the door, past whispering, snickering classmates. When I passed the desk of Rheay

Walling, a school-bus riding, country boy whose pimples themselves had pimples, he smirked and whispered loud enough for me to hear, "Now, ye goan git it."

On my way to Mr. Goodhart's office, I inventoried all the things I had done recently that might be considered a violation of school rules. Yes, I had smoked; but only outside behind the auditorium, a designated smoking area. I had not been late to any classes, and I had no unexcused absences. Yes, I had kissed a girlfriend in the stairwell before classes started that morning; but we both made sure no one could see us before we did it. Just as I reached the office door, a certain event came to mind—an event that had taken place during the lunch break merely an hour before. *Surely, that could not be it,* I thought, trying to persuade myself.

Mr. Goodhart's secretary, a serious, no-nonsense woman not much older than I, glanced up as soon as I opened the door to the principal's outer office. Without uttering a single word, she directed me toward a vacant chair next to the wall. She didn't even ask my name. I viewed this as a bad sign, a very, very bad sign indeed.

Ten minutes or more passed before I heard Mr. Goodhart call his secretary on the intercom and ask if I had gotten there yet. When she told him I had, he instructed her to tell me to come on in. She did it without smiling or speaking. She simply looked at me and nodded at the intercom on her desk. I got the impression she did not converse with the doomed.

I slowly opened the door to his office and peeped in, all the while wondering how I was going to tell my mother about whatever it was I was going to have to tell her about. "Mr. . . . Mr. Goodhart," I stammered. "You wanted to see me, sir?"

Mr. Goodhart, a handsome man with a face and demeanor to match his name, did not answer me right away. I stood in front of his desk, waiting and listening to my heart pound.

Finally, Mr. Goodhart looked up. "Young man, I just got a phone call."

I swallowed. "You did?" I managed to say, my voice trembling, my knees starting to knock.

"Man from City Stadium."

"City Stadium?" I asked, thinking about the men's restroom and the new graffiti on its recently painted walls. While I had not written anything on them, I knew who did. *Oh, Lord,* I thought.

"Well, he's out at the stadium. He's with the carnival that's setting up out there. The one's that bringing Sally Rand to town. Their drummer's taken ill, and they've got him over at the hospital. They need somebody to fill in for him tonight. Someone told them about you—that you played the drums. Think you might wanna do it?" For the first time, Mr. Goodhart smiled at me.

I smiled too, only more broadly. "Would I?!" I replied, almost shouting, so relieved was I to hear that I was not there to undergo punishment.

"He said to tell you they'd pay you . . . I think he said thirty dollars and that'd include a rehearsal at four o'clock this afternoon and the shows you'd be playing for this evening."

I couldn't believe my ears! I was going to be playing for Sally Rand, the great fan dancer! And I was going to have better than a front-row seat. I imagined myself on the stage, beating my drums and cymbals while she danced and teased, all right there in front of me, just a few feet away. And she would be naked! Naked as a jaybird! *Man, oh man*!

I was quite certain I would achieve a status among my peers accorded only to high-school quarterbacks. I would be the envy of every wicked-minded, lust-filled male in high school—which meant every boy there. Well, maybe not the preacher boys.

Mr. Goodhart wrote a note excusing me from class the rest of the day so I could be on time for rehearsal. I rushed back to Miss Snipe's room. While she read Mr. Goodhart's note, I hurried to gather up my books and, whispering, informed the inquisitive around my desk of the startling good news. They appeared dazed and amazed. Before rushing home, I retrieved the note from Miss Snipe, who sat slack-jawed in her chair, patting her flat chest.

The instant the front door slammed shut Mama yelled from the back of the house, demanding to know who was there.

"It's just me, Mama," I said.

"What's wrong?" she asked. "Are you sick or something?" She sounded worried.

I went to the back bedroom, a room my brother and I shared. I found Mama, ironing clothes and listening to gospel music on the radio. The room smelled of starch and hot cotton. "No, ma'am," I said, throwing my books onto my bed, "I'm okay."

Mama, her face drawn and tired, set the iron down and wiped away with the back of her hand the sweat that glistened on her forehead. She angled her head sideways, not smiling. "Then, how come you home? You in some kinda trouble?"

"Nome. Not anything like that. They let me out early so I can go practice," I mumbled.

All of a sudden, I began to see a problem developing on the horizon, a problem neither Mr. Goodhart nor I had anticipated. A problem I think Miss Snipe, a friend of my mama, must have seen right off. I picked my drumsticks up from a shelf, dropped them into my pants pocket, and turned to go.

Mama reached and turned off the radio right in the middle of "Turn Your Radio On." "Practice?" she said. "What kinda practice?"

"Band practice."

"Band practice? This isn't football season. And the band's had its spring concert already." I felt Mama's eyes peeling away, layer by layer, my defenses.

"It's the Sally Rand Band," I muttered. "Out at the stadium."

Mama flinched like she had seen a haint. "Sally Rand Band? You mean the one that plays for that stripper?"

I attempted to put a better face on things. "I don't think she's a stripper, Mama. I think she's justa fa . . . a . . . a dancer." I left out the word "fan" on purpose.

"You mean you're gonna be playing for Sally Rand!?" The tone of her voice bespoke shock and disbelief.

"Yessum. Mr. Goodhart, he didn't act like nothing was wrong with me doing it when he told me about it and what they wanted and all."

Mama's eyes grew wide and her forehead wrinkled. "He didn't?"

"Nome. If he did, he didn't say nothing about it."

Mama stood there for a minute, her lips tight together. Suddenly, she leaned toward me, her face just inches from mine. "Don't you go to Tabernacle Church?"

"Yes, ma'am."

"Don't we all go there?"

I could feel Mama's hot breath—breath hotter than the surface of her iron—swat my face. "Yessum," I said.

"Don't you go to Tabernacle Church?" she said, repeating her earlier question, only this time she spoke louder than before and our faces almost touched.

It finally dawned on me what she might be getting at.

"Mama," I said, "are you trying to say no, I can't go do it?"

She smiled and brought herself upright. "No," she said in a voice sweet and soft, "I'm not saying no, you can't do it."

My hopes soared. "What are you saying, then?" I asked.

In a flash, Mama's eyes blazed as she got right back in my face. "I'm saying *hell no*, you can't do it!"

In Mama's presence, I telephoned Mr. Goodhart and told him of her decision. He said he understood and promised to contact the carnival people and let them know I wasn't coming. He went on to say that he was confident they would work something out and for me not to worry.

I felt awful about not playing for Sally Rand and about letting her and the carnival people down. I also felt embarrassed. Here I was, eighteen years old and still under my Mama's thumb. I entertained no doubt whatever that I would be the object of much ridicule at school the following Monday, especially from Rheay Walling and the rest of the country-boy numskulls he hung around with.

To minimize my embarrassment and to demonstrate that I had some measure of independence, I resolved to see Sally Rand's show that evening. After all, Mama only said I couldn't *play* for Sally Rand. She didn't say anything about my not being able to *see* her perform.

"Mama," I said, "I'm gonna go on back to school. If I hurry, I can still make last period. I'd hate to miss my physics class if I don't have to."

I cared nothing for physics. I really wanted to see if I could find someone willing to go with me to see Sally Rand.

Mama, no doubt suspicious of my new fondness for a course I had straight D's in, pointed her iron toward my drumsticks. "All right, but you just leave those things right where they are. They're staying there until that woman leaves town. You understand me?"

I nodded. "And Mama, if you don't mind, could I skip supper tonight and have the car? Before Mr. Goodhart said something about me playing for Sally Rand, I had kinda planned on getting me a date and going to the picture show this evening." I told Mama the truth. I had planned on doing this before Mr. Goodhart called me into his office.

Mama sighed. "Well, I reckon so. Your daddy, he called from the plant and said he'd be late getting home. Said he had to drop off some Dr. Peppers somewhere and ice them down. I hadn't planned on fixing anything but grits and fried baloney nohow." She inserted a pants leg into the narrow end of the ironing board. "You be home by eleven. Don't you make me have to worry. You've already upset me enough to last a month."

"Yessum."

"Who you dating?"

"I dunno. Not yet, I don't." I really didn't. I just knew it wouldn't be the girl I kissed in the stairwell, or any girl for that matter.

My "date," if he could be called that, turned out to be Shorty Askew, a baby-faced munchkin with about as much sense as he had height. Among my close friends at school who did not have a real date that Friday evening, Shorty was the only one qualified by age for admittance to the Sally Rand show.

All the way to the stadium where the carnival had set up its tents and rides in the parking lot, Shorty talked of nothing but what he hoped to see of Sally Rand. He practically foamed at the mouth when he talked about her. "Let's don't walk 'round none now when we get there. Let's go straight to where they got her show set up, okay? I wanna try and get us a front seat."

That suited me. I hoped to see what Shorty hoped to see too.

The smell of parched peanuts and cotton candy greeted us as we arrived at the stadium, well before Sally Rand's scheduled six o'clock show. Our hearts sank. A long line of men stood outside her show tent, laughing and telling dirty jokes.

Above the entryway to the tent hung a huge, brightly colored canvas sign that depicted a nude woman holding two large fans that covered her private parts. The sign advertised Sally Rand as "Her Sexellency" and proclaimed her as "The Greatest Fan Dancer of Them All." Several large black and white photographs of a longhaired, young blond in various sensual poses sat upon easels next to the ticket booth.

Shorty and I strode to the ticket window where a man with greasy, black hair greeted us with a gold-tooth smile. He leaned forward and peered down at Shorty. "Hey, Pee Wee. Where's your stroller? Back off."

Shorty didn't budge. "I'm eighteen."

"Yeah," he said, "and I'm Dwight Eisenhower."

"I tell you, I'm eighteen," Shorty insisted.

The man held up a roll of blue-colored tickets. "Buddy, if you're eighteen years old, I'll eat all these here."

Shorty tossed him his driver's license and the price of admission. "Then you better start chewin'."

The man studied Shorty's license for a moment and handed it back to him along with a ticket. "It probably ain't yours." He squinted at me. "You with him, Hot Rod?"

I nodded and gave him my money, reaching over Shorty's head to do it.

The ticket seller smirked. "Enjoy the show, Baby Snooks. You, too, Hot Rod."

The moment I got my hands on the admission ticket a feeling of guilt swept over me. Usually, when I got that feeling, an admonition my mama must have told me a thousand times flashed through my brain. This time was no exception. It went: "Be sure your sins will find you out."

Shorty pulled at my arm. "Would you look how long that line is? We'll be lucky to even get us a seat."

Before we could turn to go to the end of the line, a man standing next to a concession stand near the entrance announced that everyone with a ticket could now come inside. Shorty and I sprinted forward, gave the man our tickets, and raced into the tent. We found seats on the front row, right in the middle, just a few feet from the stage.

Shorty kicked at the sawdust beneath our feet and slapped me hard on the thigh. "Ain't nobody gonna believe we got up this close. I betcha we see somethin'. Whatcha wanna bet, huh? Hot diggety dog!"

The tent soon filled with whooping, whistling, and hollering males of all adult ages. Even a few women ventured inside, their presence serving only to make things seem more exciting, but also more illicit.

Right at six o'clock, the emcee of the show, twirling a cane and dressed in a purple zoot suit and large polka-dot bowtie, strolled out onto the stage and tapped the microphone two or three times with his middle finger. He began his part of the show by insulting two men in blue overalls who sat down front to our left. "Hey fellas, you can't sit there. As ugly as you two are, you might scare the feathers off Sally's fans and that'd ruin her act." He threw them each a large, brown paper sack. "Here. Do her favor, will you? How 'bout wearing this during the show."

Both men dropped the sacks over their heads. The crowd laughed.

The emcee aimed his cane at the two men. "Would you look at these guys, everybody? They pay good money to come in here to see a buck-naked woman and what do they do when they get inside? They put a bag over their heads."

The crowd roared as the two men yanked the sacks off and looked around with sheepish grins on their faces.

After cracking more jokes for ten minutes or so, the emcee surveyed the audience with his hand held flat against his eyebrows. "Is there anybody out there who made it past the third grade? If so, how about raising your hand and letting me see it?"

Shorty raised his.

The emcee squatted at the edge of the stage and stared down at Shorty. "Why, if it ain't Little Beaver. Or is it Henry Chicken Hawk?"

Little Beaver and Henry Chicken Hawk were names of two comic strip characters.

"Listen up, Sweet Pea," the emcee said, standing and using the name of yet another comic strip character, "I asked for somebody who made it *past* the third grade, not for somebody who's *in* the third grade." The man motioned to Shorty. "Oh, what the heck! Come on up here, little fella, and let me take a gander at you."

Shorty did not have to be told twice. As the audience applauded, he jumped from his chair and bounded up the steps to the stage, smiling from ear to ear.

The man cocked his head. "You sure you're old enough to be in here, sonny boy?" He glanced over one shoulder and then the other. "You wouldn't want the sheriff to lock me up for contributing to the delinquency of a minor, now would you?"

"I'm eighteen. How many times I gotta tell y'all?"

"Eighteen months?"

"Years."

"Is that right?" The emcee took a step backwards and gave Shorty the once over. "By the way, how's the law suit coming?"

"What law suit?" Shorty asked.

"You know, the one you brought against the city for building the sidewalks too close to your butt."

More laughter erupted from the audience.

"Tell you what I'm gonna do for you, little fella. I'm gonna give you a chance to make you some money right here and now. I'm gonna sell these boxes of candy I got here to all those folks out there, and I'm gonna let you carry the boxes out to those who buy them and collect their money. For each box I sell, I'm gonna give you five cents or a nickel, whichever you want. Which do you think you might want, a nickel or five cents?"

"Five cents."

The emcee crooked his head and tapped himself on the temple. "You're a smart little devil, ain't you, son? Can't fool you. No siree bobtail. You know five cents is more money than a nickel, don't you?"

The audience laughed.

"Can be." Shorty pulled at the waist of his pants and grinned. "One of them might be a 1943 copper penny and, if it is, I'll be rich. Give me pennies. I don't want no nickels."

The emcee eyed Shorty and shook his head. "Uh-huh," he said and pointed toward the front entrance. "See that man way back yonder, Sweet Pea? The man you gave your ticket to? He'll settle up with you when we're through. Keep track of the number of boxes and don't you try cheating me, cause I know how many we got to sell. You got all that?"

Shorty nodded and hitched his trousers. "Got it."

After shooing Shorty off the stage, the man took hold of the microphone. "Ladies, if I can call you that. Any of you ever been called that before?" He paused and looked out over the audience. "One of you? Okay. *Lady* and gentlemen, each one of these boxes just might have a valuable prize in it, in addition to the best candy you'll find anywhere." He put his ear next to a box and jiggled it. "Several of these might even have a seventeen-jewel Bulova watch inside it. Just think, for only fifty cents, you might get lucky and win a watch worth a hundred times that. Now, who wants to buy a box and take a chance?"

Several hands flew up and Shorty dashed off with the candy boxes. After several minutes when it appeared no one else wanted to buy any more candy, an olive-skin man with a Yankee accent, shot up from his front-row seat and yelled, "I got one! Look, everybody!" he cried, waving a watch around. "A Bulova! A Bulova watch! Wow!"

A score or more hands pierced the air and Shorty scampered to take them their boxes and grab their money before they could realize they'd been had.

All during the candy sale, I sat wondering where the band was that would accompany Sally Rand. I saw a band stand, but it stood empty. *How was she gonna dance if she didn't have a band*? I asked myself.

A little past six-thirty, the emcee and the microphone disappeared, the lights in the tent dimmed, and a spot light dotted the stage. Shorty had not returned to his seat. I figured he had gone to settle up.

"Ladies and gentlemen," a voice announced from offstage, "for your evening's entertainment and coming to you straight from Hollywood, California, we are proud to present Her Sexellency, the star of stage, screen, the Ringling Brothers Circus, the Golden Gate Exposition in San Francisco, and the Century of Progress World's Fair in

Chicago, the greatest fan dancer of them all, Salleeee, Sally Rand! Let's hear it for Sally!"

His pockets bulging, Shorty plopped down beside me just as the applause died away and the speakers on each side of the stage began blaring an upbeat, scratchy recording of *Swinging on a Star*. As if by magic, a pretty woman not much taller than Shorty donned the spotlight, twirling two long, pink feathered fans as she took short, twisting steps around the stage in rhythm to the music.

Shorty nudged me.

"Quit it," I said. "I'm watching Sally."

He nudged me again. "What?" I whispered, trying to follow Sally's every move, hoping to glimpse a forbidden area.

"I gotta tell you something."

"Tell me later." I said, my eyes glued on Sally.

"I can't. While ago, when I went to get my money . . ." His voice trailed off as Sally spun closer to where we sat.

Shorty began again, his voice louder. "Just now, when I went—"

"Shhhhh!"

"You know who's standing out there by the drink stand where we come in at?"

Gusts of cool air put in motion by whirling fans licked my face as I sat wide-eyed, watching Sally gracefully gyrate, watching her fans turn, watching for anything I was not supposed to see.

"Do you?"

Sally pranced to the edge of the stage, twisting, spiraling, teasing. I strained to see everything I could. All at once she turned sideways, jerked her head backward, flicked one heel upward, and rolled her fans to one side—the side nearest me. It was then, between the turn and a quick tilt of the fans, that I saw something she never intended for me to see. I saw what I can only describe as her "nudity"—covered over with a body stocking.

"I seen your daddy."

"What?!"

"Yeah. I seen your daddy and he said to me, 'How'd you get here?' I told him I'd come with you."

My heart quit beating. My lungs emptied of air. "Why'd you ... why'd you tell him that for, you idiot?"

"I dunno. I just kinda let it slip. I didn't mean to."

The spotlight followed Sally Rand as she circled to the other side of the stage.

Meanwhile, I looked for me a safe way out. I couldn't face Daddy right then. What really worried me was I knew he would tell Mama where I'd been. Daddy never kept anything from her.

That same evening I sat in the kitchen across the table from both parents. They looked at me with eyes ablaze but said nothing.

The silence ended after what seemed like forever when Mama unloaded on me. "Didn't I tell you your sins would find you out? Didn't I tell you that? I don't think I'll ever get over this," Mama wailed "Thank the good Lord your daddy was out there collecting for those drinks and ran into Shorty when he did or you just might've gotten away with this, young man. Told me you had a date. You lied to me. That's what you did. Well, mister, you've had the last date you're gonna have for a long, long time, I tell you that, and when you do get to date again, you're gonna have to walk cause you're sure as heck not getting the car. So, don't you even bother to ask for it."

I had no defense. My parents had me dead to rights.

Daddy lit a Lucky Strike, leaned his chair back on its hind legs, and pointed his cigarette at me. "Thing I wanna know is how you got by me? I kept waitin' for you to come out."

"I crawled out under the back of the tent."

Smoke curled from Daddy's nose and mouth. "But why'd you do that? Shorty'd done told me y'all'd come together. Why didn't you just come on out and admit what you done like a man?"

Mama answered Daddy's question before I could address it. "Why did he run from you, is that what you mean? I'll tell you why come he done it. 'The wicked flee when no man pursueth.' That's why come."

"Well," I said, "I knew y'all'd probably be mad and—"

Mama snorted. "*Probably* be mad? That's not the half of it."

"If it'll make any difference to y'all, I didn't see nothing."

Mama heaved a sigh. "That doesn't make any difference. You looked at her, hoping to see something, didn't you? And what does the Bible say? 'Lust not after her beauty in thine heart'? Plus, you went there knowing full well you weren't supposed to." She stood and batted the air to clear away Daddy's smoke. "You know what you gotta do now, don't you?"

"Nome." I really didn't know and I feared to ask.

"Come Wednesday night prayer meeting, you're gonna march yourself down to the front of the church and you're gonna make a public confession of your sin, that's what you gonna do."

The news jolted me. "Oh, Mama, you—"

"Don't you 'Oh, Mama' me and don't you look cross-eyed at me neither. You're gonna do it, by George. Not only have you gotta get right with me and your daddy, you gotta get right with the Lord."

I scratched my head. And after I confess, then what?

I stood near the chancel, waiting my turn to confess to the members of the Tabernacle Church my sin of watching Sally

Rand do her famous fan dance. I dreaded the moment. Since my conversation with my parents on the previous Friday evening, I could think of little else than of what lay ahead for me at the Wednesday night prayer meeting. I had no idea what I would say, if I was able to speak at all.

Fortune smiled on me. When the preacher, Brother Bobby Flowers, invited all sinners who wanted to confess their sins publicly to join him down front, a Wednesday night confession veteran, Miss Eufaula Burnside, got there first. Her appearance brought groaning and grumbling from both sides of the sanctuary and cries of "Not her again." I overheard one woman remark to the person sitting next to her, "She just does it to get attention." A strange way to get attention, I thought.

In recent weeks, Miss Burnside, a frail, bony, single woman with graying red hair, had confessed to playing a card game with her six-year-old niece, reading a horoscope in the morning newspaper, overeating at the church picnic, and taking a cough medicine that contained alcohol. Miss Burnside deemed no sin too small to confess. "Sin's sin," she would say, before launching into her declaration of wrongdoing.

Miss Burnside stood crying and twisting a lace handkerchief as she waited for Brother Flowers to take his seat on the chancel behind her. She wiped her tears away and began speaking in a low, hushed tone. "Brother Flowers, sin's sin. I wanna say to you and to the Lord Jesus and all y'all here tonight, I want y'all's forgiveness of my sins. I want everybody to know I went to the picture show Tuesday night. I didn't pay no attention to what was playing, if y'all can believe that. I really didn't. I just walked right up to the ticket window and bought my ticket. I didn't know it was a Fred Astaire and Ginger Rogers picture till I got inside and set myself down. It was a musical. I can't remember what the name of it was. All I know is it showed a whole lotta dancing. I sat right there and watched them do it. Dance, I mean. I saw them holding on to each other and him swinging her all around and making her dress fly up, showing the top of her legs and all.

"I know it's a sin to dance. And even though I didn't dance, I watched them do it. I hate to say it, but I kinda enjoyed it. I guess that makes me guilty by association, me sitting there and all, watching it like I did and enjoying it. I want y'all to know I'm sorry, and I hope all y'all forgive me. Next time I go to the picture show I'll mind what's playing. I think I've learned my lesson, least I hope I have. You gotta pay attention to what you're doing all the time cause if you don't do it that ol' devil, he'll reach right out and grab hold of you before you know it and he won't turn you loose neither. Thank y'all. I'm sorry. I really am."

When Miss Burnside turned around and faced Brother Flowers, he motioned for her to return to her pew. Sobbing, sniffling, and dabbing at her eyes, she meandered up the aisle, pausing every few feet to steady herself. Only after Miss Burnside found her seat on the next-to-last row and I became the center of everyone's attention did Brother Flowers, gesturing at me with his head, signal that it was now my turn.

Miss Burnside's confession gave me an idea. I would simply follow her lead. After all, it appeared to have worked for her well enough.

With my heart beating a hundred miles an hour, my head bowed, and my shoulders lowered, I stood in front of the pulpit with folded hands. Once my nerves settled, I took a deep breath, raised my head, forced a smile, and stared out at the congregation.

A variety of faces stared back, some of them scowling and others smirking. A few people appeared sympathetic, but numerous ones—mostly children and teenagers—appeared amused. My big-mouth buddy, Shorty, looked like he always did—half asleep.

Mama, with one leg swinging and her arms crossed, and Daddy, with an arm around Mama, sat on the front row, staring nails at me.

"Brother Flowers," I began, as several of the older people leaned forward in their pews and cupped their hands to their ears, "like Miss Burnside, I, too, watched somebody else dance the other night. I hope everyone'll forgive me for doing it—like you did Miss Burnside a while ago. Thank you."

I stepped toward where Mama and Daddy sat, their mouths hanging open.

"Just a minute, son. Wait up. Tell it all," I heard Brother Flowers say from behind me in an even, gentle voice.

"Sir?" I said, stopping in my tracks.

"Tell it all."

My heart started up again. "Yes, sir," I said with a grimace.

I returned to my former position. "Like I say, I saw somebody dance the other night. They danced to that song *Swinging on a Star*. But I didn't see no dress fly up or nothing—you know, like Miss Burnside did. And didn't nobody have their hands on them or nothing." I paused, smiled a weak smile, and shrugged. "That's about it, I think, Brother Flowers. I'm real sorry I did it."

"I said tell it all, son. Where'd you see this?" This time Brother Flowers' voice was raised and insistent.

"Here in town, sir. There was a lotta people there watching it with me, but I don't guess that makes it right, though. Like I say, I'm sorry."

"Son, you gotta tell the details. We wanna know the name of the show. What was it? Where was it? Was it the same one Miss Eufaula said she saw?"

"No, sir."

"Then tell us all about it. Don't leave out anything. You know, when you pay for a loaf of bread, they don't give you a half of loaf. They give you a whole loaf. When Jesus died on the cross for your sins, He paid you for a full confession, not a half of one."

I looked at Mama. She made a face and mouthed the words "Go on. Go on."

"It was the . . . uh . . . the . . . uh . . . the Sally Rand Show," I muttered.

Brother Flowers wagged a heavily ringed finger at me. "Talk up. Can't nobody hear you. Whose show you say it was?"

"Sally Rand," I said in a louder, clearer voice

Brother Flowers bolted from his chair, a hand to his heart. "You mean . . . you mean, that . . . fan . . . fan dancer wo . . . woman?" he sputtered, his round face now the color of an over-ripe watermelon. "You talking about that woman with them fans what runs around on the stage naked as can be?" he shouted as mothers and fathers fought with their children to cover their ears.

I thought of the body stocking Sally Rand wore. "Well, she wasn't really naked. Least not when I saw her, she wasn't."

Brother Flowers' upper lip curled and he laughed. "Okay, then, what was she, if she wasn't naked?" he roared. "Did she have on a dress?"

"No, sir," I said.

"A skirt and blouse?

"No, sir."

"A shirt and pair of slacks?"

"No, sir."

"Oh, sweet Lord!" I heard Mama exclaim.

Brother Flowers rubbed his chubby hands together and smiled. "Tell us," he said, almost in a whisper but loud enough for all to hear, "was she wearing her unmentionables?"

"Her unmentionables?"

"Her drawers, young man! Her drawers!"

"No, sir. She was—"

"Then she *was* naked! Just like I said," he shouted. "Naked! Naked! Naked!"

A loud gasp erupted from the front pews and, like a rushing wave, surged backwards toward those seated in the rear. Women began to fan themselves so furiously that they produced a sound not unlike that of a flock of pigeons taking wing. All at once, a chorus of "I've never!" blurted from the throats of women throughout the sanctuary. Five or six men, on their feet, pointed accusing fingers at me and yelled, "Shame! Shame! Shame!" Several mothers grabbed their children and hurried them out of the church, ignoring cries of "I wanna stay."

I turned toward Brother Flowers when the tumult subsided. "Can I please go now, sir?"

He collapsed into his chair, removed a golden, silk handkerchief from the breast pocket of his double-breasted navy-blue suit, and wiped the sweat beads from his face and balding head. With a faint wave of the hand and a barely audible "Yes, go," he dismissed me.

As I took my seat, almost everyone gazed at me with mean and angry expressions. I felt as though I had a terrible disease of some kind, like leprosy or TB. Mama and Daddy refused even to look my way and Daddy inched closer to Mama when I sat down beside him.

After the service, the father of the girl I had smooched at school the day Sally Rand came to town met me on the sidewalk in front of the church. "Boy, lemme tell you something," he said, jabbing me in the chest with his finger. "Don't you never, ever, even *look* like you wanna date my daughter again.

You hear me? I ain't gonna have her datin' some kinda ol' sex fiend. I thought you was Christian."

The girl and her mother stood behind him, hands on their hips and nodding their approval.

I managed to free myself from the irate trio and started to hunt for my parents who had stayed behind to make additional apologies on my behalf. The last I saw of them they stood with Eufaula Burnside, hugging and kissing her and telling her how proud they were of her and how much God loved her.

Shorty caught up with me before I could find Mother and Daddy. "Shorty," I said, "you know what's happened? Do you?"

He shook his head.

"I go to church. I get up down front and I make a public confession of my sins. Do folks forgive me? No, they don't. Why one man, he comes up to me and says I can't date his daughter no more and then he calls me a name. Calls me a sex fiend. I ain't no sex fiend."

Shorty stared at me a second or two. "Yeah. And you know what else? Wasn't none of them pennies I got for helping that man sell candy that time a 1943 copper either. Not a one."

At first, I thought Shorty didn't catch on to what I had said. But then I realized that he did. His response to my complaint about the reaction I got to my public confession of sins was his way of saying that we had both fanned out.

Sally Rand fanned out herself on August 31, 1979, exiting the world stage at age seventy-six due to heart failure.

Sally Rand never knew me, but my brief encounter with her taught me an important lesson about confession. I realize 1 John 1:9 and Proverbs 28:13 teach us that confession is good for the soul, but whoever said *public* confession is good for the soul never got up and did it in front of a bunch of people at a prayer meeting—not with his mama making him do it, he didn't.

Following my experience at Tabernacle Church that Wednesday evening, I resolved that, from then on, I would confess my sins the same way that King David said in Psalm 32:5 he would confess his: "I will confess my transgressions unto the Lord."

To that I would add, "And unto nobody else!"

The Healing Touch

by Susan Alvis

We are healed of a suffering only by experiencing it to the full.
—Marcel Proust

Aunt Agnes is the self-proclaimed healer in our family. Agnes was famous for making mustard-and-rosemary cold compresses and she invented a sure cure for errant warts.

There were many folks in and around Raymington who declared her to be a walking miracle worker with an ordained touch.

Now before you go to thinking that Agnes was one of the overly educated women in the family, you need to remember that she married my Uncle Clyde when she was seventeen. They started having babies and didn't stop until my Grandmother's old home place had three children in each of the upstairs bedrooms and twins sleeping on the screened-in porch, weather permitting. Granny was long gone by then. Agnes said she died of natural causes: a combination of fatigue, boredom and ninety-eight years. How someone could grow bored in that house of bedlam is beyond me. I'd guess age had the most to do with it.

Agnes and Clyde's prolific family additions made my own

mamma and daddy convinced they would stop after one manageable child: me. I grew up in the outer orbit of my aunt and uncle's much larger family, fascinated by the noise and chaos. I am convinced, though, that I went to nursing school because of Aunt Agnes and her healing touch. We didn't have any other medically minded folks in the family.

By the time I went to nursing school in Durham, Agnes was in her late fifties, and Clyde was somewhere between seventy-five and wrecked. The more worn down old Clyde became, the more enthusiastic Aunt Agnes became about inventing medicines to treat what ailed him.

My aunt sang as she mixed the remedies that made her famous and treated people right out the kitchen door.

Now before you get to thinking that Doc Pritchard might've resented the competition or that Joe Richman down at the pharmacy didn't like that meddlesome woman, you need to remember that Agnes had worked her healing powers for both of them, so they were agreeably silent.

Joe had such smelly feet as a younger man that his dear sweet wife, Acanthus, told him he was to leave his shoes on the porch. She made him wash his feet before each meal and bedtime. Most folks around here believe it's on account of Agnes and Acanthus creating the habit of this prescribed, ritual foot washing that all four of the Richman boys became preachers, living their lives in Christ's service, washing the feet of the masses, so to speak.

Doc Pritchard's problem was halitosis. He would go to examine someone up close and personal like, and many folks just keeled right over from the odor of it all. It got to the point that he handed his patients the smelling salts before he opened his mouth.

When Agnes was done, Doc smelled slightly pepperminty and the odor of dried lavender wafted around Joe in a cloud.

Agnes cured gout with sunflowers, ulcers with coconut milk, and shingles with tar and feathers. Her concoctions got more outrageous as the afflictions in the community grew. There were rumblings of concern, but remarkably, no one died. Plenty of people felt enough better that Agnes stayed busy with a cross section of the populace so diverse that the Junior League from over in Raleigh asked her for a few recipes for their new fundraising cookbook's chapter on healing herbs.

Pauline Morris and her husband Cane were despairing over their inability to conceive. Aunt Agnes had them eating pickles and peanut butter, using Karo syrup to sweeten their tea and saying prayers. Aunt Agnes always prescribed lots of prayer.

Even though my relative was renowned for her healing touch, Uncle Clyde had some reservations about enduring the unusual cures he watched her concoct for other folks.

My uncle didn't see anything wrong with hiding a stash of aspirin or taking a long draught from a discreet silver flask of Black Jack Daniels.

This system of dealing with daily headaches and sneaking an over-the-counter rub for the occasional arthritic pain in the hip worked well for my uncle. His personal self-medicating plan suited him just fine, until a pain in a more private sector proved more than Clyde could manage on his own.

Uncle Clyde, dressed in overalls, a big floppy straw hat and black plastic sunglasses, came in disguise to see Doc Pritchard about a raging case of hemorrhoids. He swore me to absolute secrecy, and as a nurse, it was my promise to help aid in the solace of patients without causing them further pain. That very promise to cause no harm drove me out of the exam room into the hall during Clyde's check-up.

This was my attempt to save my uncle some scrap of dignity as much as to spare myself a humiliating and indelibly imprinted vision of the naked hindquarters of a relative on my psyche.

"Look here, Clyde," I heard the Doc say, as he snapped off his gloves and opened the door to let me in, "I can give you some cream that will help with your pain a little bit. You're going to need surgery to straighten your problem out. Why don't you go on home and tell Agnes what's going on. Call me back and we'll schedule a visit with the proctologist in Summerton for early in the week."

"I'm not telling Agnes anything!" Clyde retorted. Then he pointed a long, gnarled finger at me as I cleaned up the exam room, "And neither are you, Missy! There's some things sacred to a man, by damn, and if I was supposed to tell a woman what I got, then I'd have *HER*aroids and not *HIM*aroids! It ain't nobody's business but my own."

I put my right hand up, my fingers in the Girl Scout promise. Then I crossed my heart.

"Okay, Clyde," said the Doc, "Take this script and have it filled. It's a cream-based salve with a little bit of painkiller in it. Be liberal with it, and it should help."

"What's the liberals got to do with this?" groused Clyde, "A good Republican can have a pain in the arse without politics figuring in!"

"I mean use a lot of it, Clyde," Doc said, "You can always have it refilled."

I rolled my eyes at the Doc and we ushered Clyde out into the sunlight. That, I thought, should be the last I heard about that.

I was so wrong.

After work that afternoon, I went straight to the pharmacy. I needed some Covergirl and had an invitation to try something new.

Clyde came strolling in right before I left. When he got there, a crowd was eating ice cream at the soda fountain watching a woman with three shades of red hair demonstrating makeup for Mary Kay.

Every single person in the store asked my uncle a question about Agnes. He was beginning to look a little desperate when Joe glanced over the high pharmacy counter and noted the perspiration dribbling down Clyde's face.

"Hey, Clyde," hollered Joe, "C'mon back here and help me with something, will ya?"

Uncle Clyde slipped to the back between the shelves of medications. He palmed the script to Joe and stood awkwardly out of view from the sales floor. I could not help but eavesdrop.

"Look, Joe, I am not talking to Agnes about this! There's no telling what cure she'd come up with and besides that, a man is entitled to keep his business, his business!"

Joe mixed the medication, a white creamy substance, and put it in a small non-descript jar.

"Do you have a shaving kit or drawer that Agnes doesn't go through?

"Yeah, I got a case with some shaving cream and a secret jug of menthol Deep Heat that I use on my sore hips. She hadn't found that, so I'll put in there."

He left the store with his purchase in a White Knight's Pharmacy bag and walked right by me without speaking.

For three days, Clyde treated himself without much difficulty. The night before he planned to slip over to Summerton for his surgery, lightning took out the big oak tree at the side of the house and squashed his truck like a bug. He called Doc Pritchard's office and filled me in.

"Okay, Missy, now what'll I do?" Uncle Clyde asked.

"I got only one chair I can sit down on now, and I have to lean on my left cheek to do it. I'm not sleeping and you have no idea the pain I was in after I ate Agnes' TexMex and cheese-grits casserole...Damn near killed me. I tell you, I was peering down that long tunnel with a light at the end!"

A lighted probe extended down a dark tunnel was what Doc Pritchard had recommended in the first place, so I suggested he just tell Aunt Agnes or call the proctologist and explain his transportation problems.

Now before you get to thinking that I should've given him a ride, Uncle Clyde had already made it a personal policy not to ride anywhere with anyone else. He either drives, and drives his truck, or he doesn't go. This has been his self-proclaimed traveling credo since all his children have been on the earth. To church? Aunt Agnes made two trips in the old Bonneville station wagon, dumping the wee ones in the nursery before returning home for the teens and tweens. Uncle Clyde drove, with great dignity and parked his truck right next to the preacher before waiting for Agnes at the door. I could've offered him my old VW, but I would've only incurred his wrath.

The proctologist's office gladly rescheduled Clyde's appointment, but the earliest date was set for three weeks out.

It was after midnight, five days after the storm, when Agnes roused me from sleep, crying helplessly into the phone.

"I can't help him," she cried, "And he is on the floor, crying like a child! Be honest, Missy, is he dying and hasn't told me?"

I was wildly uncomfortable and very tired, so, I passed the buck, trying really hard not to break my oath to Uncle Clyde.

"Look, Aunt Agnes, I know for a fact that Uncle Clyde's not dying. Why don't you call Doc Pritchard?"

"I did! I did call the Doc! Their housekeeper said that he and Elmira have gone to the symphony and a romantic weekend in Raleigh and won't be home 'til Sunday."

"Okay. I know the Doc gave Clyde a prescription of cream for his, er... ah, ailment. Find his medicine and let him use it. He knows what to do. It's personal. That's all I can say. Aunt Agnes, I promised."

There was a silence on the line and then she said, "I will not forget your unwillingness to help him, Missy. I can forgive, but I may never, ever forget."

I drove straight to their house. Agnes jerked open the door, stomped right through the house and stood next to Clyde who was writhing on the rug. I wavered, hanging back in the doorway to their bedroom.

"Where's your medicine, Bub? Sweetie?" she said with softness. "Let me help you. I've seen it all and after going through childbirth in the double digits, unless you're getting ready to birth triplet bowling balls, there isn't any pain I can't help you through."

Uncle Clyde pointed to his shaving kit and said, "Hand me the little white jug. I got 'roids, Agnes! Bad, wicked 'roids. There are flaming torches stabbing me from my rear end to my inner stomach. I know if I could stand to get my pants down, you'd see the smoke from the fire! I'm dying here, I tell you, dying!"

Agnes handed over the little white jar he indicated and I retreated from the room to give them some privacy. I went to the kitchen where I brewed some rosehips tea, stirring in a hefty dose of cooking sherry. Then, I returned to the door of the bedroom.

"I need help," Clyde called. "I gotta have some help!"

I put down the mug of tea and opened the door. I carefully touched his brow and said, "Let her. Let Agnes nurse you now."

Aunt Agnes used the entire contents of the jar before Uncle Clyde began to really feel a deep, burning response to her ministrations. He began a sing-song, guttural moan.

Agnes packed his bottom full of smelly white cream. She used every last dab of the self-heating menthol rub that Uncle Clyde had been sneaking to use to penetrate his achy arthritic joints.

When the heat began to permeate the raw tortured membranes of Uncle Clyde's heretofore unmentioned recesses, he plumbed new depths of pain.

"Woman!" he bellowed, "Dear, Sweet Lord, take me to heaven now, 'cause the fires of hell are burning up my rear!"

I drove them to the Emergency Room so that I could explain to the physician on duty all that had transpired. Uncle Clyde was weeping unabashedly, his anguish beyond measure.

He was in so much agony that he didn't even notice that his attending physician was a beautiful young woman named Geraldine Powers. My uncle might have just died on the spot had this fact registered through the flames of hell in which, he was positive, now fully engulfed his nether regions.

First, Dr. Powers knocked Clyde out with a shot for pain and carefully washed away the smelly cream of doom. Then she irrigated my Uncle's angry orifice.

Aunt Agnes excused herself to the hospital chapel. I followed her down the hall and sat on the back pew while she bargained with God.

Aunt Agnes, talked plainly. She and God seemed to be good friends. She approached her prayers like a discussion with a confidante. Then, she made a deal.

"Lord, You and I know that the credit and joy I have so willingly taken for healing the sheep in Your flock is a source of the greatest pride in my life. I will own the sin of this pride. If you will heal my Clyde, Lord, I will promise to give *You* all the healing glory. I will never, ever mess with the health of any of your other children with any chemical or natural manipulations that may lead someone to believe I know what in heck, pardon my French, I'm doin' Father. Also, forgive me for pretending that pickles helped with the baby making process. They were all I had in the fridge that day and I just gave the Morris couple what I had. I appreciate Your omnipotent ability to make twins from peanut butter and old cucumbers. You are a mighty God, and I may have taken that for granted. I give you my word of honor...My healing days are done. Amen."

By the time we returned from the hospital chapel, the doctor was having a Eureka! moment of her own.

"I haven't seen anything like that since medical school," she said, "when one of the women in our class accidentally put Colgate in her diaphragm instead of spermicidal jelly. She was blistered inside for days."

I may be a nurse, but this was information that I could have done without. I couldn't think of a mental medical category to place it in.

"The unusual thing is," she said, "the heating attributes of this particular menthol rub appeared to have opened, and then chemically cauterized, the affected tissues. When he wakes up, he'll be sore for a day or two, but his hemorrhoids should be gone. I would ask that he see a physician, straight away, should this problem return. And I further encourage you to never, ever suggest this healing process to another living soul on earth."

The doctor really pressed this last bit of information on Aunt Agnes. Then she finished writing in Uncle Clyde's chart, leaving us to keep vigil by his bed until daybreak.

When Uncle Clyde woke up, he stretched, before remembering the excruciating pain that had dominated his life for the last memorable days. That he was feeling better dawned across his face with a relieved grin, followed at once, by his familiar scowl.

"Agnes? Can you ever forgive me? You healed me. If I had just come to you in the first place, you'd have fixed me right up, for sure," Clyde said.

I cleared my throat, letting him know there was audience present.

My Uncle glowered at me. "What'er you a doin' here?"

"Clyde," Agnes said, sweetly, "I called Missy because I knew she would have a modern perspective on my healing arts. She told me what your medicine looked like, not what it was for...don't you remember? You told me yourself where I should put it."

Weeks later, I was sitting on Aunt Agnes' porch, visiting with my cousins and drinking long swallows of sweet, mint tea. Uncle Clyde pulled up in his new Chevy truck and climbed the front steps to perch on the edge of the porch.

"I gotta come see the Doc, Missy," Clyde said, massaging his knee, "Need something else for this tinge of artheritis. I've used that whole jar of white stuff he gave me, and it ain't worth a hoot!"

Did he really think hemorrhoid cream *could* work on arthritis?

"Don't look at me," said Agnes, looking back at me. "Me and God have an understanding. You can explain the healing contents of that jar if you want to, Missy. I am now officially retired."

The Hope Quilt

By Susan Goggins

"Hope" is the thing with feathers—
That perches in the soul—
And sings the tunes without the words—
And never stops—at—all
—Emily Dickinson

"Let me help you, Grandma." I reached past my grandmother's arthritic fingers, my hands stretched above hers to retrieve the folded quilt on the top shelf of the plain cedar chiffarobe. We had gone in opposite directions for so long—I growing taller, she shrinking with age. But it still surprised me as a teenager that I had become bigger and stronger than this woman who to me was always larger than life.

I put the still-folded quilt onto the bed she'd shared with my grandfather for over fifty years. The bed in which she'd borne my father. In the simple farm house where her husband had been born as well. "The friendship quilt," I said. "I remember you showing me this when I was a little girl."

I ran my hands over the seams holding the fragile-looking pieces together. I said, "You and some of your friends all pieced a bunch of quilt squares, then got together and quilted them so you all got a quilt like this." I'd remembered reading about friendship quilts. The quilting bees were social events complete with refreshments and probably lots of gossip.

"Is that what you thought?" Grandma asked. She laughed. "This ain't exactly a friendship quilt. It's what I call my hope quilt. You know what a hope chest is?"

"Sure. That's where a girl would sew and embroider her household linens and collect them in a cedar chest so that she would be ready to set up housekeeping with them when she eventually got married." It was the seventies then, the years of women's lib, and such old-fashioned ideas seemed positively prehistoric, but I'd never tell Grandma that.

"That's right," Grandma said. "A girl worked on all those linens, acting on faith that she would eventually get married and be able to use them in her own home."

"Instead of ending up an old maid?"

"Yep," Grandma said.

I smiled at what she'd left unsaid. I hadn't been as attentive to learning the womanly arts of cooking and needlework as she had been. I think she despaired of the younger generation of females in general. My mother had taught me to embroider some and Grandma had taught me to tat a little, but the shuttle didn't fly like it did in her hand. For me, lacework was a pretty awkward business, and I ended up pulling the wrong thread and tying my work up in knots as often as not. I could make picots and join them, but not much else.

"I want you to have it," Grandma said. "It brought me luck and maybe it will for you too."

Touched, I clasped it to my chest. "I'll treasure it, Grandma." I leaned forward to kiss her cheek, fragrant and dry with her favorite face powder. "So why do you call this the hope quilt?"

"Do you remember how I said that a girl filling up a hope chest was an act of faith? Well, when I was a teenager, World

War One was just ending in Europe, and who knew if all the boys who had gone were gonna be coming back."

I put the quilt back on the bed and followed Grandma into the kitchen. It was a half-hour before supper. Time to make the biscuits. She opened a deep drawer next to the sink and took out her ever-present bowl of self-rising flour. She'd attempted to teach me to make biscuits as patiently as she'd tried to teach me to tat, so knowing all the steps I went to the refrigerator and fetched the two-pound package of Snow Cap lard. I'd heard part of this story before.

"Wasn't the Spanish flu epidemic killing a lot of soldiers who were waiting to be sent home from Europe?" I dipped out a couple of tablespoons of lard into the tiny iron skillet Grandma kept on top of the stove and turned on the burner.

"I was worried plumb to death about your Grandpa," she said, measuring out some milk in a tiny glass she used only for the purpose of biscuit making.

"And I guess the other girls in the community were worried that what with the war and the flu, they might not be able to find husbands," I said.

Grandma poured the milk into the middle of the bowl of flour and paused a moment for it to sink in. Then she stuck her fingers into the goo and started swirling the stuff around in a circle, gathering up flour as the dough started gaining the proper consistency. "You bet they were. So was I. I hadn't seen your grandpa in two years, and I didn't know if he'd remember me or not."

"Shaw," I said. "I expect he couldn't forget you." I laughed, scooped up some of the cold lard out of the box and smeared it onto the biscuit pan.

"Well, I wasn't so sure." Grandma got the skillet by the handle with a potholder, or "hot rag" as she called it, and carefully spooned some of the melted grease into the biscuit dough. The rest would be dribbled on top of the biscuits to bake them a perfect, golden brown. My mouth was about to water already. "I'll admit I was worried about the competition," she said. "I knew of at least two other girls in the community who had their eyes on him."

I watched her swirl some more flour, which was kind of hypnotic and relaxing. "So how did he come to pick you?" I asked.

"That's an interesting story, and it all started with that quilt. It was really your Grandpa's, you know."

"Your hope quilt belonged to Grandpa?"

"It started out that way." That's when Grandma, still swirling and swirling, took up the rest of the story.

Ben's mother, Anna Grace, was making a quilt to give to him when he came home from the war. She asked all his aunts and girl cousins to make a square and sign it in India ink or embroidery, and of course, she made a square herself.

When she asked me to make him a square, I was tickled to death. That was, until I heard that she asked Myrtle Dickens, one of them Douglasville Dickenses, to make him one too. And if that didn't cap the stack, she also asked the new Methodist preacher's girl, who just moved into the community, to make one. So I figured that was my competition, and I backed my ears for it. I had loved Ben since the first grade when he'd poured well water on my head from the gourd dipper and ran. And I couldn't let another girl steal him away.

"Myrtle was Anna Grace's cousin's, next-to-youngest girl. I knew her from the singing school, and let me tell you that girl couldn't sing a lick. Not only that but she left the vanilla out of the banana pudding she made for the dinner on the ground. So she couldn't sing and she couldn't cook, and I couldn't imagine what Ben or Anna

Grace saw in her. She wore nice dresses, though, with matching hair bows for her curly, dark hair, so at least somebody in the family could sew.

"The preacher's daughter's name was Lizzie. She was a stout girl with rosy cheeks and sandy hair. I had met her in Sunday school, and she struck me as proud. Her father had been assigned to our country church after serving in Atlanta, and I got the feeling Lizzie was a city girl through-and-through. Who knew if she could cook or sew or sing, and I didn't know what Anna Grace saw in her either.

Grandma's hands never stopped moving. "Anna Grace invited the three of us to bring our squares to her house one Sunday after dinner—you know that's lunch to folks nowadays—and get the quilting started. So when Sunday rolled around, we all showed up with our sewing baskets, and Anna Grace showed us into the parlor and gave us teacakes.

"I do believe these are the tastiest teacakes I nearly ever ate, Mrs. Grogan." Myrtle said.

"Just the right amount of vanilla," I said, looking sideways at Myrtle the flatterer, who narrowed her eyes at me.

"We get Watkins double strength vanilla in Atlanta," offered Lizzie. "It's the best there is."

"Thank you," Anna Grace said. I don't know which one of us she was talking to. "Why don't you show me your squares?"

It's hard to know what to put on a quilt for a man. I mean, you wouldn't use a Dutch Doll or an appliquéd flower. That would be too feminine. I thought about doing a log cabin block, but that was too simple to show off my sewing. I decided on a cottage appliqué. It looked nice and homey and might put him in the mind of settling down—with the girl who'd sewed it. Anna Grace put on her spectacles, looked right close at it, and told me it was good work.

Then Myrtle got out her square. Lord, if it wasn't a Sunbonnet Sue! "I made it out of the scraps of my best dresses," she said. "To remind him of me."

Well, now, that flew all over me I'll tell you right now, but I didn't say a thing. I looked at Anna Grace to see what she thought. Her mouth puckered a little bit, and she said, "Mmm hmm." Just like that. I could see she thought it was forward of Myrtle to do her square that way. A Sunbonnet Sue on a man's quilt with her own dress material in it. Law! My mama would have beat me.

Then Lizzie got out her square and you would not believe—a double wedding ring! I like to have died. I *say* it. Me and Myrtle just stared at each other with our mouths open like a couple of trout. What was the meaning of this?

Anna Grace said, "Why, that's real pretty, Lizzie. I remember Aunt Mary Nell used to do a lot of double wedding rings."

"That's what my Mama said. She said Aunt Mary Nell was y'all's very favorite aunt." Lizzie favored Myrtle and me with a glance and a little simper to go with it. "My Mama and Anna Grace are first cousins."

Well! As you can expect, I didn't rightly know what to do. I reckon me and Myrtle finally got our mouths closed by the time Anna Grace got over to her sewing machine to sew our squares, the very last three, onto the quilt top. I kept my head down, pretending to look for my quilting sharps in my sewing basket, while I tried to think of what to do.

It wasn't nothing for second cousins to marry in those days. This city girl thought she had a claim on my future husband because of family connections. The double wedding ring quilt square made that perfectly clear. I just had to figure out a way to get Anna Grace on my side.

When Anna Grace got the quilt top finished she had us help her put the top and the backing together with the cotton batting in the between. Now I can put in a quilt as tight as Dick's hatband right by myself, but with somebody trying to help me, much less three somebodies, it's a job that could make a preacher cuss, kind of like hanging curtains. You have to get everything all straight and make sure all the wrinkles are out of it and what with one pulling it one way and somebody else another, we right nigh started pulling hair even while trying to stay on our best behavior.

Finally Anna Grace got the quilt pinned onto the ticking, which was tacked to the side of the frame, and we got it hoisted onto the cords that suspended the whole thing from the ceiling. The three of us got seated in front of our squares so we could all quilt them. It was a tight squeeze. I was on one end and had to come at it sideways so Myrtle could sit in the middle. Lizzie had all the room she wanted because hers was on the end. And believe you me, she needed the room. That girl could down teacakes the way a field hand could put away collards and cornbread.

Anna Grace was going around the edges of the quilt basting it down here and there so the layers wouldn't slide. She gave us a big spool of white cotton thread for us to work with. I took it and measured out an arm's length before I bit it off and handed it to Myrtle. I reckon the fight had gone right out of Myrtle. She had done gone plumb peaked. Even her hair bow kindly hung like a sad sack. But I was still thinking, even as I threaded my needle. I was never gonna give up on your Grandpa.

Lizzie had been yammering on about Atlanta and I think she was even getting on Anna Grace's last nerve almost as bad as she was getting on mine. It was during an especially tedious description of the fine houses her father's family lived in that I got my idea.

"What line of work is your Pa's family in, Lizzie? Are they all preachers?" I asked, all innocent-like. I was doing my quilting in the shell pattern that Anna Grace had showed us on a piece of paper. She wanted it all to match.

"They're bankers mostly, all except for my Daddy, who got the call to preach the Gospel." Lizzie said, with a proud little tilt of her chin.

I thought about how my granddaddy always said he'd trust a mule trader before he'd trust a banker and smiled. I could get five stitches on my needle, using my underneath hand to guide it, before I pushed it through with my thimble. Myrtle was only getting three and Lizzie two. I couldn't tell if Anna Grace noticed. "Do you have any farmers in your family?"

Lizzie wrinkled her nose. "Not on my Papa's side. My Papa's side has the educated professionals. My Mama's people are the farmers." She was ignoring the pattern that Anna Grace had given us and was doing her quilting in some fashion that looked like a fan. A crooked fan.

"Do you fancy the country yourself?" I said a little prayer and reached into my sewing basket for another needle and some dark embroidery thread.

"Oh, no," Lizzie said. "I prefer the city." Lizzie didn't miss the way Anna Grace's thin eyebrows arched close together setting up a wrinkle down the middle of her forehead, so she quickly added, "Of course, I could live in the country. . . if I had to."

"Could you now?" Anna Grace said. She had started quilting squares opposite us.

"Well, you know, being a farm wife is hard," I said. "Why, my mama and my grandmas and all my sisters and aunts and girl cousins can plow like men. . . if we have to." I threaded my new needle with the embroidery thread and hoped I could do some free-hand script with a running stitch without making a mess of it.

Myrtle might not could sing or cook, but she wasn't slow. She looked at me keenly as she took another stitch. "Me, too," she declared.

Lizzie looked distressed, and one of her little white hands, the one without the needle in it, fluttered to her throat. It was plain she had no idea how to use her free hand to steer her needle underneath the quilt. "Really?"

"Oh, yes. To put food on the table, farm wives get to do everything from churning butter to butchering hogs. Why, my first chore on the farm was when I was four years old. My Grandma would wring an old chicken's neck and cut his head off with a hatchet on the chopping block. "My job was to keep the cats offen it until it stopped floppin'."

Lizzie turned as white as the quilt backing, and Myrtle snickered.

"I heard you were a good hand with the livestock," Anna Grace said as she kept on quilting.

I started my letters with the running stitch. I had to make it look just right. "Yes'm. I had to pull some pigs just the other day. One of them Yorkshire sows was having trouble with her first litter how they will, you know."

"W-what's pulling pigs?" Lizzie asked. Myrtle leaned over and whispered something in her ear and if Lizzie didn't stab herself with her needle, I wasn't sitting there. A look of horror came over her face like she'd seen a haint. Myrtle had just told her that I reached in after them pigs and pulled them right out. Why, if I hadn't of, they would have all died, the mama too. My arms were slim, but they were strong.

"Be careful, there, Lizzie. You don't want to go and get blood on that pretty block," Anna Grace said. If she thought my pig birthing talk was too unladylike for the parlor, she didn't let on.

Lizzie was trying to pull herself together, but she was still looking a mite bilious. It was then that she stuck out her little chin and said, "Well, Daddy's people will find my husband a job in a bank. In fact, they're opening a new one in

Charleston. That way we can live in the city and I won't have to do any of those awful things."

Well, Anna Grace showed her teeth like a mule eating briars and huffed out a breath, but she didn't say anything. Finally, she looked my way and noticed how I was stitching away like stitching was fixing to go out of style. "What are you doing there, Winnie?" she asked me.

"I'm just adding a little saying onto my square," I said. Anna Grace came over and looked over my shoulder at it. Then she patted me on the head and gave me a wink.

When it was time to go, she said goodbye to the other two girls, but put her hand on my shoulder to stop me from following. "Winnie, why don't you stay to supper?"

"I'd be happy to, Miss Anna Grace," I said. "You know, ever since I tasted your biscuits at the last camp meeting, I've been wanting to see how you make them. Would you teach me?"

My future mother-in-law hugged my shoulder a little and took me into her kitchen, where she opened a drawer and got out a bowl of self-rising flour and a tiny little glass.

By the time Grandma had finished the story, the biscuits were in the oven and she was sitting in her wooden rocking chair, the one with the flowered, homemade cushions. The long narrative seemed to have tired her, and she drifted off to sleep, a gentle smile on her face.

I tiptoed to the bedroom and unfolded the quilt. I hadn't paid close attention to the individual squares before, but now I scanned each of them quickly, looking for the one with the cottage appliqué. And there it was, on the edge next to the tattered binding. In neat, even running stitches faded with the passage of time, my Grandma had embroidered her name and the phrase, *"There's no place like home."* I laughed and refolded the quilt.

I checked on the biscuits—almost at just the right golden brown—and went back to the living room as Grandpa was coming in the door with a grocery sack in each arm. Grandma opened her eyes at the sound of the door opening.

"If it isn't my two favorite girls," Grandpa said.

I took one of the sacks and kissed him on the cheek. "Biscuits almost done," I said.

"I'll go wash up. Be right back. Don't start without me, now." We set the bags on the kitchen table, and Grandpa walked toward the back of the house.

I started emptying the bags—two gallons of milk (one sweet, one butter) a bag of corn meal, a jar of peanut butter. Grandma put the kettle on to boil. "You're pretty smart, Grandma."

"How's that?" She removed the biscuits, as perfect as always, from the oven and put them on another hot rag in the middle of the table.

"How did you know just how to get Great-Grandma on your side?"

Grandma laughed. "I had the notion that Anna Grace was wondering how she was going to keep your Grandpa down on the farm after he'd seen Paree'. She'd decided to marry him off straight away or she wouldn't have invited the three of us girls to that quilting bee. She was determined that if she ever got him home from the war, she'd keep him here. And I 'spect she figured that a good way to do that would be to have a bride waiting for him when he got back."

"You sure knew how to eliminate the competition. That cottage appliqué' looks a lot like this farm house."

"Doesn't it, though? I thought I did a good job on the porch especially."

"I would have picked you anyway, you know," Grandpa said. He'd been leaning on the refrigerator while Grandma was setting the table. "Even without my Mama's encouragement."

"Gee, Grandpa, you're almost as smart as Grandma." I laughed and took the last item out of the grocery bag—a quart jar of sorghum syrup.

"I don't know if I'm a smart man," Grandpa said, taking his place at the head of the table. "But I know I'm a lucky one."

Grandma poured boiling water over the instant coffee in her and Grandpa's cups and milk in a glass for me. Then we joined hands and Grandpa said his simple prayer of thanks for the food Grandma had prepared.

After our "Amens" I asked, "Can I make grey horse with this fresh sorghum?"

"You know you can," Grandma said.

I poured some of the thick brown syrup onto my plate and put a dab of warm butter in the center. "Why do they call this grey horse?" I asked, probably not for the first time, but for the first time in my memory. "It's not grey, even when you swirl it. It's more light brown."

"Who knows?" Grandpa said, stirring his coffee in the cup with the pinecones on it, the same cup he'd used for, by my estimation, about a million gallons of coffee in his lifetime. "It's just a country saying that goes with all the country ways we have. We say it because our folks said it to us and theirs said it to them."

"That's good enough for me," I said. I got myself a biscuit, made the same way as generations of my womenfolk did, put my knife into the butter and sweet-sour syrup and swirled and swirled.

The Sun, the Moon, and a Box of Divinity

by Clara Wimberly

It is prosperity that gives us friends,
Adversity that proves them.
—Proverbs

Summer, 1949

Mary Ann Callaway was the prettiest girl in the fourth grade. She was also the smartest. She had thick brown hair with streaks of shining blond hidden in the depths. She wore the nicest clothes, nothing handmade like the rest of us. I always envied the way she looked in her pleated wool plaid skirts and cardigan sweaters. On those cold wintry days when many of the girls in class wore pants underneath their dresses to keep warm, Mary Ann never did. She might wear woolen knee socks; she might even wear a longer dress. But she never wore those boyish pants.

I never understood why she chose me as her best friend.

My other best friend, Kay Dean, was nothing like Mary Ann. She was as poor as any kid in class. She made C's in school and didn't seem to care. But she always made me laugh. There was nothing Kay Dean wouldn't do. She was bold and adventurous and rebellious and had a sense of who she was long before any of the rest of us even knew what that meant.

Mary Ann and Kay were acquaintances but as much as I wished we could all three be best friends, it just didn't happen. I was often caught in the middle of trying to please them both.

My mother once said that Mary Ann and Kay were as different as the moon was from the sun.

I began to think of them that way. Mary Ann was like the moon—cool and elusive, sitting quietly in the distant night sky. Beautiful, but never causing a fuss.

She was the kind of girl you wanted to sit and talk quietly with. Someone with whom you could share your innermost feelings and emotions. We studied together, our laughter ladylike and subdued. With Mary Ann I felt mature and sure about what I wanted in life. I knew that she would always be my friend and that she would never betray me.

Kay was like the sun, unpredictable, either out and too warm or hidden by clouds and unavailable. The sun was bright and hot; couldn't be ignored and sometimes you wished it would go away, just for a moment of peace and quiet. That was Kay Dean exactly.

When Kay and I played together, I usually allowed myself to be coaxed into doing something I knew I shouldn't. Nothing really awful, just small forbidden things. She was the first person I ever skipped school with. The only person I ever smoked rabbit tobacco with and the first girl I heard use a cuss word. She was full of mischief, and sometimes our antics made me feel quite guilty. But she had a good heart and would do anything for me, and I knew she loved me as a sister.

The first time I spent the night at Mary Ann's house was in the spring of 1948. After the games and birthday cake, Mary Anne was allowed to have one guest stay over. She chose me.

I'll never forget that day.

To begin with, I'd never been in a house like the Callaway's. The white two-story home with large columns in front sat on a hill overlooking a narrow country road. It looked like something out of *Gone with the Wind*.

Mrs. Callaway met each guest at the door. I remember that she wore a cotton dress sprigged with pale green flowers, and she wore a pearl necklace. She was very pretty and so polite. She didn't treat any of us like children, but rather like honored guests.

She seemed so different from Mr. Callaway. He was the sheriff of the county and also a farmer. Daddy always said he was a good man—probably the best and most honest sheriff we'd ever had.

I remember seeing him drive past our house in his faded blue pickup truck on his way home. He always wore a hat, and he always chewed on the short stump of a cigar that was never lit. He was a plainspoken simple man who sounded like the rest of us.

Mrs. Callaway, although she had a southern accent, sounded different. Her speech was slower, more languid, and even more southern than ours.

"Why you must be Cara-line," she said as she welcomed me to the party that day. "Mary Ann has told me so much about you. Come in, darlin'."

I wondered if I should tell her my name was Caroline. Then as I heard her talk and greet others, I decided she had called me by the right name—it was just her pronunciation that was different. I was fascinated by her accent. Somehow she sounded so genteel and elegant.

We played games, including musical chairs in the large

living room. Our chairs were placed in a circle on a thick, lovely old rug of muted blues and greens. We were surrounded by beautiful antique furniture and lamps, and art work in gilded frames. A huge grandfather clock ticked softly in the hallway.

Mrs. Callaway had a colored lady who helped with the cooking. That day she came into the living room carrying trays of dainty rectangular sandwiches and cups of pink punch. I'd never tasted anything like it.

Kay Dean picked up several of the sandwiches, stacked them on top of one another, making a Dagwood-like serving, and tried to cram it into her mouth all at once.

Mrs. Callaway came in quietly, took Kay by the arm, pulling the sandwiches away from her mouth.

"Southern ladies never, ever make gluttons of themselves in polite society," she said. "No matter how hungry they might be."

Kay Dean, looking chagrined, lowered her eyes and took a small nibble from one small sandwich. "Yes ma'am," she said.

"There," Mrs. Callaway said. "That's much better, sweetheart."

"Do you like the sandwiches Cara-line?" she said, turning to me.

"Yes ma'am," I said. "Very much. I don't think I've had it before."

"Probably not, but it's very simple to make. It's just plain old cream cheese and watercress."

I knew about watercress because we always had it in a salad in the spring. But I didn't tell her I'd never tasted cream cheese.

"You know when I was a little girl, livin' in Mobile, Alabama, we had tea every Sunday afternoon. There would be cucumber sandwiches, watercress and cream cheese sandwiches, cheese straws with orange marmalade, and a variety of desserts."

"Mmmm," we all said, though most of us weren't sure what she was talking about.

"Cucumber sandwiches?" one of the boys said, laughing loudly. "Heck, who'd want to eat a cucumber sandwich?"

"Why, everyone loves cucumber sandwiches," she said. "Boys are silly, aren't they, girls?" Mrs. Callaway said, turning to go back to the kitchen.

"Boys are silly—boys are silly," the girls chanted. What with dainty cucumber sandwiches and watercress with cream cheese, I'm sure the boys were ready to go home.

"What's a glutton?" Kay whispered to me.

After everyone left, and after I made sure they all knew I got to stay, Mary Ann and I went to the kitchen. We sat at a small table while Mrs. Callaway and the colored lady cleaned up. We nibbled on sandwiches and cookies and listened to them talk, rolling our eyes sometimes when we didn't understand.

I hadn't seen much of Mr. Callaway during the party. But that evening, in Mary Ann's upstairs bedroom we dressed for bed, then Mary Ann took my hand and pulled me toward the stairway. Her little sister Patsy was with us, but her other sister was away visiting relatives.

"Patsy and I always go down and say goodnight to Mama and Papa," she said.

I loved the long curving stairway with its gleaming white banister and spindles. The steps were carpeted and felt good to my bare feet.

Mr. and Mrs. Callaway sat in the living room; she was sewing, and he was reading the newspaper in the glow of a green shaded lamp, the ever-present cigar still clamped in his teeth.

"Well," he said when he saw us.

"Look at these three beautiful young ladies, Mama. Where do you think they came from?"

"Why I suspect they came straight from heaven," she said, smiling at us.

Patsy and Mary Ann laughed and ran to jump in their father's lap. I stood back shyly, hardly knowing what to do and feeling a little awkward standing there in my nightgown.

The girls kissed their father and then their mother, and Mr. Callaway rose from his chair.

"Who's first?" he asked.

"Me, me," Patsy said.

"All right, the baby is first," he said. He picked her up and carried her up the stairs and into her bedroom. Then he came down, and Mary Ann stood back, nodding toward me.

"Take Caroline next, Papa," she said.

"Would you like me to carry you upstairs?" Mr. Callaway asked. He seemed very tall as he stood looking down at me.

I shrugged my shoulders, feeling very shy. How could I tell him I was afraid I was too big for him to carry?

But he scooped me up in his arms and carried me up the stairs as if I was as small as Patsy. He put me down at the top of the stairs.

"Wait here while I get Mary Ann."

He carried Mary Ann up, giving her a kiss on the cheek before putting her down beside me.

"Are you tired Papa?" Mary Ann asked. "Carrying three girls up?"

"Not one bit," he said, smiling at her.

"How long do you think you'll carry me?" she asked.

"Until you're a married lady and I'm a very old man," he said.

Mary Ann took my hand, pulling me to her bedroom. She giggled and said; "He says the very same thing every night."

Before going to sleep, I lay in bed thinking I'd never had a day quite like that one.

A few weeks later I went home with my friend Kay. Her environment was entirely different. They lived in a four-room house, not much more than a shack, really. A little ramshackle white frame house, with floors that were not quite level. The walls were paper-thin and in winter the house was freezing cold with only a large pot-bellied stove in the middle of the living room. I have seen the stove so hot that the metals sides glowed red. Still, the heat only permeated the cold in a small circular area. The rest of the house remained frigid.

Kay's mother was one of the dearest women I ever met. I often called her my second mother. Our treats after school, so different from the Callaways, were plain country food—sometimes in odd combinations. I remember that their refrigerator was practically empty except for a jug of milk (straight from the cow at the barn), a cardboard container of lard and a carton of R.C. Colas.

I was shocked when I met Kay Dean's dad. He was a sort of jack-of-all-trades, a self-proclaimed religious man, who worked with junk cars and often came in with grease caked on his overalls and hands. He had a little half smile on his face, but I had an uneasy feeling it was not genuine. He frightened me, and I knew immediately that if my dad ever learned what kind of man Kay's dad was, he'd never let me come back.

This particular day, her dad asked Kay Dean if she were wearing lipstick. Of course we wasn't wearing lipstick, she was only 9 years old. But he didn't believe her and drew back his hand as if to hit her across the face.

I gasped and took a step backwards, and then Kay's mother came in from the kitchen.

"Joe!" she said. "What are you doing? If Kay Dean says she wasn't wearing lipstick, then she wasn't."

The family attended an evangelical church. Makeup and short hair on women were strictly forbidden. As was showing one's shoulders, arms, or legs. Wearing a bathing suit, dancing, or swimming with a boy was also strictly forbidden.

But we were young, and none of these things had entered our minds yet. We just wanted to have fun.

Mrs. Jones hurried us away to the kitchen, then sent us out to the garden for lettuce, an onion and a tomato. Our after-school treat that day was a cold biscuit with mustard, lettuce, onion and tomato. Then she handed each of us a Mason jar filled with hot cocoa.

"Run along, girls, and play on the hillside behind the house. Have a picnic," she said, smiling. "Enjoy yourselves."

She was a dear, sweet woman and I loved her. I thought it was wonderful that she did everything she could to help us have fun. But somehow I couldn't get the image of Kay's dad out of my mind. The way he smiled as he drew back to hit her and the look of hurt and humiliation on my friend's face. She was afraid of him, and sometimes I think she hated him.

I'd never known what it was to fear anyone. Certainly not my own daddy. And I knew that Mary Ann had never experienced that, either.

I wished more and more that Sun and Moon, my two best friends, could one day be friends. But it didn't seem likely.

We were out for summer vacation, and I didn't see as much of my school friends. But Mary Ann lived just down the road from me, and we saw each other more often.

One day I realized I hadn't seen her in couple of weeks. And we hadn't seen Sheriff Callaway driving by in his old blue pickup.

"Maybe they're on vacation," Mama said.

I saw Daddy drive in from work and get out of his truck. He looked worried about something.

I ran out on the back porch; he was on the ground and lifted his water jug up to me on the porch.

"Bad news, honey," he said, looking up at me.

"What?"

Mama came out onto the porch, drying her hands on her apron.

"The Callaway girl is sick," he said. "They think she has polio."

I heard Mama gasp as she came and put her hands on my shoulders.

"Mary Ann?" I asked. "Are you sure it's Mary Ann?"

"I'm sure, honey," he said.

"Polio," I whispered. I remembered the frightening movie newsreels showing all the people with polio. It was the scariest word a family could hear. There were sometimes pictures in the paper of children in huge iron lung machines—horrible silver machines that looked suffocating. "But isn't that...she won't die, will she, Daddy?"

Daddy's brown eyes were sad when he looked at me.

"I don't know, honey. It's bad. They're in Hot Springs, Georgia, trying to get the best treatment they can."

"Hot Springs..."Mama said. "That's where President Roosevelt went. It must be very expensive."

I remembered seeing President Roosevelt in the newsreels. too. He looked perfectly healthy to me. I had no idea at the time how he had kept his illness from the public.

"Yes, he had a house there—remember? It's the best polio treatment center in the country," Daddy said.

In the next few days as the news spread, the community was in turmoil. People felt deep sympathy for the Callaways and for Mary Ann. But they were also afraid. At that time polio seemed to come from out of the blue. No one knew where or how it was contracted. For a while, the yards were empty of children as parents kept them inside, even in the hot days of summer. I knew my parents were afraid, too.

"I want to go see her," I said.

"Honey, that's a long, long way from here," Daddy said. "We can't go there, and besides, I doubt they'd let you see her if we could."

I went to my room and sat on my bed. I felt too sad to cry.

Mama came to the door, smiling at me sympathetically.

"Why don't we send her a card?" she asked.

"Can we?"

"Of course we can. We'll go with Daddy into town and find a real nice card for her. You can even write a letter to enclose with it if you like."

After we mailed the card I watched the mailbox for days. The mailman came around noon, and every day I'd run out, hoping to find a card from Mary Ann. But nothing came. I sent another card and then another.

A few days later, Sheriff Callaway's truck pulled into our driveway. Mrs. Callaway and Mary Ann's sister, Patsy, were in the truck. Mr. Callaway got out, walked around, and shook hands with Daddy. Mama came out, and we went to the truck.

"Hello Cara-line," Mrs. Callaway said. "I just wanted to tell you how very much Mary Ann appreciates your cards and letters. She wants very much to answer them, but unfortunately she isn't able to write at the moment." Her voice caught, and she looked down at her hands in her lap.

I looked at Mama, and she shook her head, warning me silently.

"We're all so sorry," Mama said, stepping to the truck window and touching Mrs. Callaway's arm.

"Thank you," Mrs. Callaway said, still not looking up. I saw that her face was wet with tears. "We hope...we hope that soon she'll be able to use her hands."

"She's completely paralyzed?" Mama asked, almost whispering.

"Her right side," Mrs. Callaway said. "Her left side is not as bad, and we're hoping she will be able to learn to write with her left hand." Mrs. Callaway's lips trembled, and I saw Patsy looking at her mother. Her eyes were filled with tears too.

I'd never felt such excruciating pain as I did that day when I realized what having polio really meant. This was Mary Ann we were talking about! A girl I knew so well. The calm, serene Moon. The smartest, prettiest girl in our class. To think of her helpless and paralyzed seemed impossible.

How could this be happening?

"Oh, I wanted to tell you Cara-line," Mrs. Callaway said. "Your friend Kay's mother sent Mary Ann a box of divinity fudge. Mary Ann said it was the first thing she's enjoyed since she got sick."

"Kay's Mother is a good cook," I said.

"Yes, she is, "Mrs. Callaway said. "And a good woman. She sent the nicest card and said their prayer group at church were praying for our little girl." She sniffed again, and bit her lips to keep from crying.

"People here are so good...so kind. So many of them I don't even know. And yet they are praying for us and for our daughter. I believe those prayers will bring her home soon."

The Sheriff got back in the truck.

"We just came home to get clean clothes," he said. "We'll be going back down tomorrow. I wanted to ask if you'd keep an eye on the house for us."

"Be glad to," Daddy said.

Mr. Callaway waved over toward me, his smile sweet and sad. I remembered the night he had carried us all up the stairs at their big house.

As I watched them drive away I knew that we would never experience days like that again. I ran to my room and cried until I couldn't cry any more.

In a few weeks I did receive a card from Mary Ann. The writing was odd and almost illegible but she was proud to be writing with her left hand.

"The therapy hurts terribly but everyone here is so nice," Her letter said. "The nurses help us swim in the warm water of the springs every day. That's my favorite time of day, except for mail time," she said. "So keep writing to me."

By now my friend Kay had begun writing to Mary Ann as well. And in each letter I received from Mary Ann she was sure to mention Kay and how funny her letters were. I even told her about how my mother and I compared them to the *Moon* and the *Sun*. We all laughed about that and they decided if they had to have such nicknames I would have to be a *Star*.

At last it seemed I had my wish about all of us being friends.

We knew that Mary Ann would be coming home in the fall just in time for school. But unfortunately she would not be able to attend regular school because of the braces she wore on both legs and the metal walking aids she used.

Kay and I both went to visit her at the big white antebellum house as soon as she came home.

Mrs. Callaway stood smiling at the bottom of the stairs, as we walked up, slowly and sedately, neither of us speaking. Kay Dean's eyes were huge as she gazed around at the beautiful furnishings.

We went into the bedroom and found Mary Ann sitting up in bed. She didn't look like the same girl we knew. The polio had pulled the muscles in her eyes to one side and also one side of her mouth. I wanted to cry when I saw what Polio had done to her beautiful face.

But she smiled at us and Kay and I went forward pretending that nothing was different. Mary Ann and Kay talked and laughed as if they'd always been friends while I sat quietly and listened.

Mary Ann's illness had changed us all.

We couldn't stay long because she tired easily. But as we were leaving Kay Dean turned back to Mary Ann.

"My mama said to ask if there is anything we can do for you," she said.

Mary Ann thought for a while, then her eyes brightened.

"All I could think about the last few weeks at Warm Springs was your mother's Divinity. I'd love to have some more. If Its not too much trouble," she added softly.

"Shoot no," Kay Dean said. "She'll be happy to make you some. I'll bring it over Sunday after church. How's that?"

"Great," Mary Ann said. "It'll give me something to look forward to."

"Okay. See ya *Moon,*" Kay said with a wave of her hand.

"See ya *Sun,*" Mary Ann said. "See ya *Star,*" she added giggling.

We walked quietly out the door, and then Kay elbowed me. She gave me one of those mischievous looks and started running toward the top of the stairs.

"Kay!" I hissed. "No. We have to be quiet."

Mrs. Callaway was sitting at the bottom of the steps, waiting for us. She looked up and smiled.

Kay stopped in her tracks.

"No, Kay. Don't be quiet. You girls can be as noisy and silly and girlish as you wish. The house was so quiet this summer and we were so sad. I prayed every night just to be able to hear laughter in our home again. I think you two just answered my prayers."

She stood up and opened her arms and we both went to her and put our arms around each other.

"I hope you'll both come back often."

"We will," both of us chimed.

"Thank you for being such good friends to my little girl when she needed friends most," she whispered.

Dirty Harry, the Mule

by Mike Roberts

A mule will labor ten years willingly and patiently for you, for the privilege of kicking you once.
—William Faulkner

Greg chased mischief the way knights of old chased the Holy Grail. He acted like he was on a quest to annoy, frustrate, or embarrass as many living things as possible before he turned thirteen. If a boy's lunch box was stuffed with dirty gym socks, if a girl had an "I'm on my period" sign taped to her back, if a dead opossum was found in the trunk of a car, or if a cat had firecrackers tied to its tail, Greg was the prime suspect.

If things had been different, say if Greg had been just a boy at school or down the block, I could have avoided him. I'd have stayed safe and never, ever had a run-in with that cantankerous mule. I don't mean Greg, although Grandma always said he was mulish. I mean a real jackass mule.

But I had three strikes against me. Strike one, Greg was my cousin. Strike two, my mother and her sister, Greg's mother, were so close it's a wonder they didn't wear the same clothes. I don't mean clothes that looked alike. I mean the *same* clothes. When the two of them were together, you could hardly fit a piece of paper edgewise between them. Strike three, Greg and his whole family had moved on my grandparents' farm a little ways from that mountain called Monte Sano in northern Alabama to take care of the old folks and keep the farm going.

My mamma loved that farm, so at least once a month Greg's shadow darkened my life. But I was better off than Daryl, who couldn't get away from Greg at all because he was Greg's brother. Even worse, Greg was older by a year, heavier by twenty pounds, and stronger. When Greg would concoct a new scheme—my English teacher Mrs. Bales likes that word *concoct*—he'd convince Daryl to go along. If talking didn't win Daryl over, Greg would beat on him the way Moe beat on Larry and Curly in The Three Stooges features.

Greg never beat on me, though. I'd seen what he did to Daryl, and I decided it was better to go along and *maybe* get a whipping for causing mischief than to refuse to go along and get pounded *for sure*.

Because he was usually on the giving end and not the receiving end of meanness, Greg was a happy kid. Notice I said "usually." The one frustration in Greg's life was that mule I told you about.

We'd named him Dirty Harry because he squinted like the actor Clint Eastwood did in the Dirty Harry movies. Grandpa bought Dirty Harry about the time Greg started school, and the animal took an early dislike to the boy. That mule would let Grandpa work it all day long on jobs that were too much trouble for the wheezing old tractor, jobs like dragging wagons full of hay or hauling loads of firewood. But let Greg try to get Dirty Harry to do anything, and that mule would refuse to move, or bite Greg's fingers, or swat him in the face with its tail. Once, it even pooped where Greg was standing. Greg was barefoot at the time. Why he'd be standing barefoot on the wrong end of a bad mule I don't know.

Now, Grandpa might've been old, but his mind was as sharp as that razor of his that I cut myself with trying to shave when I was nine. He knew what a pain Greg was and how much that mule annoyed Greg. Every chance Grandpa got, something like this would happen:

"Greg! Go hitch up the mule to that wagonload of feed. Take it on down there to the south pasture and give it to them cows before they go and starve themselves to death trying to eat that wire grass."

"Aw, Grandpa!"

Then Greg's mother would speak up. "Gregory Matthew Wilson, go do what your grandfather said this minute!"

"I'm going," Greg would say and stomp toward the door, cussing under his breath and thinking nobody could hear him.

Just as Greg's hand would touch the doorknob, Grandpa would say, "Son, you better watch what you're saying before I have to turn you over my knee and wash your mouth out with soap. I may be old, but I'm still big enough to do it."

"I wasn't saying nothin'."

"Yeah, and I'm the King of England. Now go on and get." Grandpa would stand at the window and watch Greg struggle with the mule. For the rest of the day, Grandpa would smile a lot.

But it was Grandpa himself that told Greg what the mule's weakness was. I'm sure Grandpa never meant to do it, like I'm sure that if Grandpa had known what was going to happen because of a slip of his tongue, he might have washed his own mouth out with soap.

The revelation came one day while Greg and I were leaning on the pasture gate and watching the veterinarian treat some of the farm's livestock. The vet looked over the cattle, then checked Dirty Harry. When the vet finished, he took off his University of Alabama ball cap long enough to wipe sweat off his bald head and turned to Grandpa.

"Y'all ever ride this old mule?"

"Ride him?" Grandpa chuckled. "Naw, he can barely stand having a blanket on his back, much less people. I don't know what he'd do if somebody tried to throw a leg over him. He might have a heart attack or something, walk a few feet and drop down dead."

A look of evil glee came over Greg's face. I figured he was concocting again, so I slipped away and went in the house. Once there, I looked out the window and saw Grandpa walking toward the house and Greg talking with the vet. Then the vet left and Greg came inside . . . and sat . . . and watched TV . . . and poked fun at the cartoons the way he always did. Nothing else happened.

After a while, I relaxed enough to go outside with Greg, Daryl and Pinkney Usher, a boy from across the road, to play World War II with slingshots loaded with BBs. I should've known Greg was up to something, though, when he volunteered to be part of the German army. Usually, Greg wanted to be an American because the Americans won the war and he insisted on winning. Somehow his new attitude went right on by me like one of his fastballs. Anyway, he was a German, and he made Daryl be a German, while Pinkney and I were the Americans.

I felt sorry for Pinkney. How two parents who seemed to love him the way they did could name him the gosh-awful name *Pinkney* or any other name that would saddle him with the initials P.U. I never understood. Mamma allowed as how *Pinkney* was an old Southern name. I allowed back at her that it's best for some old things to die off.

About a half an hour later, Pinkney's mother hollered across the road for him to come home and try on some new shoes she'd bought him. The rest of us declared a truce and rested in the grass. I was the only one with a BB wound, and Greg volunteered to go in the house and bring out a bandage for me. This time his generosity set off an alarm in my thick head.

When he came back and handed me a Band-aid, I asked him, "Greg, how come you're being so nice?"

Greg was spared the need to decide whether to tell the truth when Pinkney ran over to show us his new leather slip-ons. We just nodded at them, and he looked hurt. Pinkney was raised in a house full of girls, and I wondered if he expected us to carry on about those shoes of his like girls would have. He was strange that way.

"Hey y'all," Greg said, "you want to really have some fun?" He yanked a big, red bandana from a back pocket of his jeans.

"Yeah, sure!" Pinkney said. Pinkney was a bit dim, as well as strange. Daryl and I gave each other a narrow-eyed, "What's Greg thinking?" look.

Greg led the way to Dirty Harry, who was standing at the pasture gate nibbling at the thick grass that had so far escaped the lawn mower. Dirty Harry stopped munching, looked past Daryl, Pinkney, and me as if we weren't there, fixed a cold eye on Greg and went back to nibbling.

"Y'all stay here a minute," Greg said. He clambered over the gate rails and disappeared into the nearby barn. He emerged carrying a feedbag in one hand and that bandana. The evil glee was back in his face when he stared at Dirty Harry and said, "Here, you old jackass, you hungry?"

He climbed the rails again to get high enough to reach the top of Dirty Harry's head and slipped the strap of that feed-bag over that old mule's ears. Dirty Harry shook his head only once in protest before attacking the feed in the bag. The mule was so happy at having an unscheduled snack that he forgot he was meantempered. Greg tied the bandana over

Dirty Harry's eyes and pushed Dirty Harry's body parallel to the gate rails, but Dirty Harry didn't even snort.

Greg looked at the three of us. "The vet told me about blindfolding and feeding an animal to get him to do what you wanted. OK, now y'all climb on."

"Climb on what? That?" Daryl said, his face frozen in an expression of disbelief that could've been lifted off a comicstrip page.

"That's right. We're going to sit on ole Harry."

"He's really tall," I said in my way of trying to say no without actually saying no and risking a pounding. "How are we supposed to get on?"

"Climb up the rails and swing a leg over the old puke's back, that's how," Greg said.

Daryl shook his head. "I don't think Grandpa wants us riding his mule."

"We ain't going to ride him. We're just going to sit on him a minute, all four of us." When Daryl didn't start moving, Greg added, "And if you don't hurry up, I'm going to slug you one." Daryl climbed. So did I.

That left Pinkney on the ground. He held up a hand about head high, his face pinched. "Greg, I can't go climbing fences in these new shoes. My mother will kill me if they get scuffed."

"Well, take them off, stupid." Greg paused, his expression changing to a sneer. "That is, unless you're yellow. Pink, you ain't yellow to sit on a mule's back, are you?"

"N-n-n-no."

"Then climb up!"

Moments later, we were all on Dirty Harry's bare back. Daryl was in front because Greg ordered him to sit there. Greg was right behind Daryl so he could hit him if necessary. I slid on behind Greg. Dirty Harry's back was so wide that stretching my legs over it made my muscles hurt. The mule's backbone, which stuck up about three inches from everything else, poked my underwear into places it shouldn't have been. I looked down from that mountain of a mule and saw the ground about a half-mile away. I got dizzy and grabbed hold of Greg's belt loops.

"What are you doing? You ain't scared, are you?" Greg said.

"No, I'm fine," I lied. I was about to lie again and say how much fun this was when Pinkney got on behind me and locked his arms around me. It was hard to breathe for a while after that.

Daryl turned so he could talk in our direction and said, "We've sat on him, now let's get down."

"Give me my bandana first," Greg said. Daryl hesitated before untying the bandana and handing it back to Greg. Dirty Harry shook enough to make me and Pinkney holler, then settled down.

"All right," Greg said, "push the feed bag off his head."

"I ain't going to do that," Daryl said. "That'll really make him mad. You know better than to take food away from a big animal."

Greg jerked forward, and I heard the sound of a fist hitting flesh. Daryl yelped. "Now do it or I'll hit you again, you chicken."

I peeked around Greg and saw Daryl push the feedbag until the strap slipped off the mule's head. The feedbag hit the ground with a thump. Dirty Harry shook again, snorted, looked back at us and bent its head down to nuzzle the feedbag.

"You've fed your face enough, you big old pig," Greg yelled. "Now geddup!" He kicked his heels into Dirty Harry's flanks. The mule brayed.

"Hey! Stop it, Greg," Daryl yelled.

"You said we weren't going to ride it!" I yelled.

"So I fibbed," Greg said and kicked again. The mule brayed louder and took a few steps. "Yeah, now go, stupid, and drop down dead."

At Greg's third kick, Dirty Harry sprang forward like a whole nest of hornets had stung his rump. He headed across the pasture at gallop.

"Yeehaw," Greg yelled. "Grandpa said he'll be dead in a minute. Ain't this great?"

Greg was welcome to his opinion, but I thought I was being beaten to death. Dirty Harry's strides were throwing me into the air and dropping me onto that sticking-up backbone as Greg and Pinkney slammed into me from front and back. All the spankings I'd ever gotten put together wouldn't have been that bad. After fifty yards of mule ride, about the only parts of me that weren't numb were my head and feet.

Worse, I was losing my grip on Greg's belt loops. Once I thought I'd lost it altogether because my hands flew in the air. Then I realized that they were still hanging on and went in the air only because Greg did.

I'd heard about people becoming paralyzed with fear, and before getting on Dirty Harry I thought I knew what that meant. But I hadn't. Now I did; I couldn't seem to make anything work. I couldn't move unless the mule made me move, and I couldn't decide whether it was better to stay on or jump off. Staying on meant pain. Falling all the way to the ground that was blurring past the toes of my tennis shoes also meant pain.

"I thought you said he'd be dead by now," Daryl said.

"Shut up!" Greg hollered.

The mule went faster and turned to run along the pasture's west fence. Barbed wire, fence posts, trees and undergrowth whipped by a few feet away.

Pinkney screamed, "I'm going to wet my pants!"

I found my voice. "No you're not, neither. Not on me."

From in front, Daryl hollered and Greg let out a string of swear words, some of which I didn't know he knew. At first, I thought Greg was mad at Daryl. But the pitch of Greg's voice got my attention. He wasn't mad. He was terrified.

I couldn't help but stretch tall enough to see what would make Greg show fear. I wished I hadn't. A few feet inside the fence line was a huge oak. One of its limbs was slightly more than mule-head high off the ground, and Dirty Harry was running straight at it. In a few seconds, that old mule was going to use that limb to flick us off his back the way he'd use his tail to flick flies off his backside.

"Turn him! Stop him! Do something!" I yelled, but I'd already decided it would have taken God himself to make that demon mule change his mind or his direction.

When we were maybe thirty feet from the limb, Dirty Harry ducked his head to make sure he didn't get knocked cold. But Daryl was holding onto Dirty Harry's mane, and got pulled forward and down enough to put his head into line with that limb. He screamed, and I didn't blame him. I could also see that even if we didn't all get our heads knocked off, we were going to get some broken ribs or busted insides from getting hit by that limb or flying boys. I had figured out what I had to do when Greg confirmed it.

"Jump! Jump!" he yelled.

Daryl was the first one off. He catapulted into space like a rock from one of our slingshots. Greg probably threw him off. Greg went next, slinging his arms to one side to give him momentum, but I still had my fingers wrapped around his belt loops and Pinkney still had me around the middle. I felt enough of a jerk to pull me sideways, then my hands were free and Pinkney and I were coming off the mule in slow motion.

In the air, I heard lots more screaming, felt Pinkney let go and thought how tall the grass looked as it came at me. I hit so hard on my stomach that my ears rang and I couldn't breathe or see or even feel much for an instant. I knew I slid forward and rolled over once, maybe twice. My body started working again, and I felt pain all over as if I were one, boy-sized bruise. My face was stinging, and when I touched it I pulled away a bloody hand. I whimpered as I tried to find out where the blood was coming from, and I didn't care who heard me.

But I doubt Daryl and Pinkney could have heard, because Greg started shrieking. When I saw him I knew why. His left forearm, which should have been straight, had a bend in it between his elbow and wrist that looked like the bottom part of an "S." Eyes bulging, he held that broken left arm in the right one and ran toward the house, his ripped belt loops flapping.

Daryl was on all fours, tears running down his face and groaning, "My butt's broke. My butt's broke." He tried to stand, fell on his side, yelled and flopped over on his front.

"What happened to Greg?" I called.

"He musta landed on his arm," Daryl replied.

"Try to stand up again," I said. "If you can, you're butt ain't broke." He struggled upright and was able to limp over to where I was.

"You know you've got a bloody nose and a busted lip?" he said. I nodded.

Pinkney was behind me crying, but not from pain. Daryl and I investigated and saw that of the four of us, he had the fewest wounds, at least to his body. His pride was much worse off. The back of his shirt, his arms, his neck and the seat of his pants were caked with wet, smelly manure.

"Eeeuuuuu! Guys, get this stuff off me." He gagged, and I moved away in case he threw up. He didn't. When all of us were on our feet, we started toward the pasture gate. Daryl and I made sure to keep Pinkney downwind of us.

Dirty Harry headed toward the gate, too, since the barn was in the same direction. A few yards ahead of us, he stopped, turned, snorted and caught us in that Clint Eastwood crooked squint as if daring us to ride him again.

I looked at him, feeling like the punk the real Dirty Harry had whipped. "I guess we went and made your day, huh?" I told him. Dirty Harry threw his head back and brayed until we drew even with him. Satisfied, he trotted off toward the barn.

By the time the three of us reached the house, Greg had already left with his mother to go to the emergency room to get his broken arm set. Grandma, Grandpa, my mamma, and Pinkney's mamma met us at the gate. Grandma already had a washcloth and a bucket of water, and after making sure Daryl wasn't cut up or broken up, started cleaning blood off my face. Mamma and Grandpa stood side by side, staring at us boys. Mamma shook her head in disgust while Grandpa choked back a laugh.

Pinkney's mother, seeing he wasn't hurt, yelled at him for losing his new shoes. He was trying to tell her he'd left them in the grass by the gate when she got a whiff of him. She turned pale and led him to the backyard hosepipe to wash him down and strip off his fertilized clothes. Grandpa brought soap.

Greg spent the rest of the day in the emergency room and came home with a plaster cast that ran from his knuckles to his shoulder. That, an old-fashion belt whipping, and two months of being on restriction kept him out of mischief for a while. He wasn't deprived, though. After two days at school, he had signatures all over the cast and the phone numbers of three girls who felt sorry for him. I never did understand girls.

Daryl got a stern talking-to for having gone along with Greg.

He didn't get a whipping because Grandpa allowed that the boy had had enough punishment.

Mamma lectured me while driving me to the emergency room to have my lip seen about. The doctor gave me two stitches.

Poor Pinkney had to walk home wearing only his now-wet underwear and a blanket Grandma threw around him so he wouldn't be indecent out in public.

Dirty Harry won the battle of the ride but lost a bigger battle—the one between the sexes. Not long after our misfortune, a friend of Grandpa's had a female draft horse for sale. Grandpa bought her so he could keep up with his plowing and such when Dirty Harry wasn't in the mood to work, which was often.

I guess because old Harry hadn't shared the same pasture with anything close to his own kind for so long, he decided he liked her, even if she was bigger than he was. But she, being a good judge of character, wanted nothing to do with him. If he came too close to her she'd snort and bite and kick at him. After a couple of weeks of that, Dirty Harry kept to himself and sulked.

That made me feel sorry for him, but only a little.

Mommy Darlin'

by Debra Dixon

Were they really there, whispering wordless
encouragement to her, or was this part of her dream?
"Whether you are there or not," she murmured sleepily,
"good night—and thank you."
—Scarlett O'Hara, Gone With The Wind

Y'all know what a hellmouth is, don't you? It's a dandy little term I learned from my extensive study of *Buffy the Vampire Slayer*. Think of a hellmouth as the convergence of dark forces. A horrific concentration of evil in the midst of sunny southern California. An evil that can only be battled by Buffy, the Chosen One. One tiny teenager against all the world's evil.

To my way of thinking, Buffy—and California—got off easy. What's a vampire or two compared to raising a son in the South? What's sitting on a hellmouth of evil compared to not having a maternal bone in your body while sitting on the hellmouth of maternalism? Because the South is nothing else if not maternal.

Think of me as Scarlett surrounded by modern-day Melanies, women who are born knowing how to nurture. Women who have created the legendary sons of the South. Women who make you feel inadequate at something as simple as kissing boo-boos. (Yes, that's an art form in the South. Takes years of practice. You have to start with dolls and move on to baby cousins, which are usually plenteous.) I never played with dolls and had no baby cousins.

That shouldn't have mattered. I had the "Mother Of All Mothers." The woman could bring a bad handyman to his knees while simultaneously diapering an infant, churning homemade ice cream, and bottle-feeding an orphaned newborn hound dog. I was *supposed* to get those genes. I didn't need to *practice*. I was Southern, from a long line of Southern.

How hard could motherhood be?

We are often foolish when we are young. I didn't know that when the time came, I'd be flying by the seat of my pants and that all the stress and friction of motherhood would catch my damned pants on fire. If I had known, I'd have paid more attention to motherhood practice.

Instead, I frittered away my practice years, eschewing dolls and boo-boo kissing for puzzles, books and kick-the-can. Why play with dolls when you could be out playing an advanced hide-and-seek game involving an empty beer can, older boys, and the heroic rescue of your "jailed" friends? All of this misspent childhood added up to an independent, fairly intelligent (all those books), not-so-sentimental adult.

Then what did I do with all that intelligence? I promptly married a Southern man who thought seven children would be a lovely-sized family. Fortunately, size was negotiable. We decided to get pregnant and play it by ear. The Saint (as he was, and still is, dauntingly called by all) was thrilled; I was worried. How in Heaven can you live up to the inevitable comparisons with a man referred to as a saint? I knew who our children were going to love and it wasn't me.

Suddenly I regretted leaving Chatty Cathy out in the rain and pulling the arm off the ancient Betsy Wetsy. Neither accident was a particularly good omen. I wisely kept those omens to myself.

Really... who among us would actually admit publicly they suck at motherhood? In the South, it's tantamount to saying, "I don't know how to make sweet tea." The whole room gets real quiet and people swivel to look at you with mouths agape. The Women's Circle at the church pats your hand while saying, "Bless your heart."

That might *sound* kind but that phrase is usually anything but kind. It's more the kiss of death. You find it preceding the blunt horrible truth of a situation. As in: "You haven't met JoElla? Bless her heart. Poor girl. If she fell in a bucket of butt-ugly you'd never be able to find her again."

So instead of confessing my embarrassing lack, I turned to books, my friends of yesteryear. By the time the little baby made an appearance, I was ready to attend to any possible physical need and could quote long passages of baby psychobabble. I could spout all the important Southern truisms:

"The best birth control for a first date is ratty underwear."

"Beer is not a food group."

"Make sure the deer in the back of the SUV is really dead before you start the drive home."

Regardless of whose yardstick you used, I was ready. Still, as we left the hospital with a blue bundle, I said a little prayer and asked God to steer me clear of redneck territory. Redneck tendencies crop up all too often in the South. I was worried. Especially since our son, William Richard, had a name which was perilously close to "Billy Dick." To make matters worse, his father was fond of flannel shirts and cowboy boots.

I don't mean to criticize rednecks. It's just that I'm not a redneck kind of girl. I'm white-bread middle class. I don't like Confederate flag bumper stickers, shirts with the sleeves ripped off because it's hot outside, ball caps with permanent ring-around-the-crown, gun racks in trucks, or beer cans rattling around the floorboards.

Today, twenty-one years later, I am proud to say my son is only three-fifths redneck. (His truck has no gun rack and his beer cans make it to the trash.) If I had to attribute my success in the redneck area to something specific, I'd credit the pie chart—although I didn't know at the time the chart was an anti-redneck charm. I just thought it was the best way to do the "mommy job."

Everything I'd read said that babies like a familiar routine, a schedule. Well, that's great in theory, but babies are way too young to do the job of scheduling themselves properly. So, I analyzed the kid's waking, sleeping, and eating times. Next, I juggled feedings a little here, a little there, until his longest sleeping period was at night. Easy as pie charts.

I know because I made the pie chart. Color-coded. It's in his baby book.

Did I mention that I'm intimately acquainted with overkill? I only know how to do something 120%. And that's how much I loved that baby from the first moment I saw him. In the second moment, I realized that I'd have to be a better person if I wanted this incredible little creature to love me back. Compared to the Saint, I was a shallow, selfish twit.

The good news was that I had nowhere to go but up.

I thought sons loving their mothers was a given. Half the newspaper advice columns you read are about a wife who's mad because her husband still has apron strings attached to his belt loops. Besides everyone knows sons aren't like daughters. Sons don't become unhinged during their teenage years and hate their mothers for no apparent reason.

Heck no! In the South, sons clash with their fathers. In the South, you aren't a man until your daddy says you're a man. It's all about the Daddy. Saint or not, tradition is strong. I thought I was safe. All I had to do was a reasonable job of it, go to every soccer and baseball game I could, and teach him to say *please* and *ma'am* and put *Miss* in front of ladies' names. (I don't care how many times you've been married in the South, you're still *Miss* Betty if you aren't actually related, but are important to a child.)

Yes, indeedy. All I had to do was raise him to be a strong independent young man, who respected women for having brains as well as boobs, and he'd thank me for it. Maybe even love me back.

It seemed like such a good plan. A doable plan.

I made it through the baby years without a problem. Except for that incident with the car seat. Yep. That was bad. No getting around it.

I'll never forget my pride at being ready to take that first outing, just me and the baby. I loaded half the nursery into the trunk of the car, packed two diaper bags, and buckled him into the car seat. It really is a shame that I didn't buckle the car seat into the *car.*

I can tell you from personal experience that when you turn a corner and hear the unexpected thud of tumbling baby and car seat, the only two thoughts in your head are:

Huh...what was— oh God, please let him be okay!

and

His daddy is going to kill me.

While you're thinking these thoughts, your body is functioning on muscle memory. Your hands steer into the first parking lot your eyes locate. No thought goes into it. You just do it. I ended up in the parking lot of a little gro'.

A *gro'* is a dying breed of non-franchise, mom-and-pop,

get-your-pickled-eggs-from-a-big-old-jar-on-the-counter, country grocery store. They dot the smaller towns and feeder highways leading into the cities. You'll even occasionally find one with warehousing and industrial sprawl grown up around it. A gro' left standing in a city has either cheap beer, simple-but-good eats for lunch or both. This little gro' seemed to have had both, judging from the crowd.

There were ten or twelve of them that day. Rednecks at lunch with beers in hand. I count myself lucky. There could have been thirty standing there pointing and rushing over to see why I was praying so hard and flinging car doors open to get to the baby.

The guys were a little puzzled about why I was carrying on so and jiggling a happily slumbering baby to wake him up. Bill cracked one eyelid as if to say, "Hey! Cut it out. I'm trying to get a nap here!"

When I started crying in shaky relief, they thought I'd been overcome by the stress of motherhood. As I painfully explained that I'd been overcome by an attack of stupidity, I heard a chorus of snickering and a couple of outright guffaws. Then being good Christian men, they sobered up and tried to offer comfort.

"Well, bless your heart." A tall, forty-ish man offered. He wore faded denim you had to earn, not purchase. He pulled a pouch of Redman from his back pocket, got himself a pinch, and said, "You ain't very good at this, are you? But don't you worry. This ain't no problem."

Another good ol' boy stepped up to add his helpful two cents. "That's right, ma'am. He's right. Your little Bubba'll be okay. Hell, I been puttin' my seven in the back of my truck since they was knee-high to a grasshopper with nary a problem."

Faded-denim guy nodded at the baby, "He don't seem to mind."

Right on cue, Bill threw up on my shirt.

Et tu, Bubba?

As Bill grew past toddler-hood, which was a miracle given my lack of maternal instinct (see car seat story above), we taught him life skills, convinced people not to call him Billy Dick, and patted ourselves on the back for a job well done. We taught him to cope with mosquitoes and humidity, how to fish (despite my redneck reservations) and gave him structure. Well, *I* did that last part about structure because the Saint doesn't do discipline or confrontation other than to say, "Yes, your mother is right." (The Saint may be irritating but he is not stupid.)

We figured we'd done so well with this one, we ought to stop at one. Sort of quit while we were ahead.

It wasn't until Bill was about twelve that I began to suspect my lovely plans for a doting son and perfect parenthood were going awry. The day was gray and wet and ordinary except for the nasty cutting wind. We'd played dozens of soccer games like this. He trotted in from the muddy field toward the bench, face smeared with bloody-nose residue, rain, snot, mud and grass bits. I walked over to tend his wounds, and he shrugged me off.

His meaning was quite clear. Mom not required, *thankyouverymuch.*

"Hey, coach," he said. No urgency. No emotion.

"Yo?"

"I don't want to play goalie next half."

The coach came over and summarily looked at the mess on Bill's face. "You injured?"

"Nah." Bill pulled up his jersey to his forehead and wiped casually downward, blood and all. "Too much pressure."

Coach snorted dismissively. "Then suck it up, boy, and get the hell back out there."

I bristled at the coach's tone and language, but Bill shot me the look before I could intervene. You know "the look." The one that says, "I've got this covered." I stumbled to the bleachers and plopped down. Stunned by my superfluousness. Where was the child who wanted only Mommy when he broke his leg?

Apparently, gone with the wind and toting a soccer ball to kick off the next half.

Shortly thereafter, on a night that will live in infamy, I finally made the trip back from the land of denial. I realized that the legendary attachment between mothers and sons was just that—a legend. There is no guarantee. In one heart-stopping moment the future became clear. I was going to be in a nursing home at ninety-four with no one to come and visit me unless Bill married and I managed to make his wife adore me. (And, honestly, what are the odds of that happening?)

In one defining moment of my motherhood, I realized that my son would go blithely off to his own life in a few years with nary a thought of me or a Mother's Day card coming my way. My son's wife certainly wouldn't be writing to the advice column about her husband doing too many chores for his mother. If I did get a Mother's Day card, she'd be the one writing it.

How did I know all of this in one moment? I'd better start at the beginning...

The Saint travels. A lot. I've never managed to adjust to being alone in the house when he's gone. I know I'm a grownup but it's just not something I can do—sleep well if I'm alone in a house. Especially in an old house. Our house is an old house. It makes noises. Creepy noises. The kind of noises that have you carefully peering out your bedroom door and down the hall for evildoers.

Plus we have trees. The kind with long branches that tap the windows and make eerie screeching-scrabbling sounds against the glass. Or drop magnolia cones on your roof. There is nothing like a thud to make you bolt upright in bed when you're alone.

The cats don't help. They come sit in your lap while you're watching TV and then peer oddly over your left shoulder as if there is a serial killer standing behind you. You turn to look and there's the shadow of...of *something* so you gasp, throw the cat, and run for your life before realizing you've been "had" by the cat again. Then you have to hunt down the cat and torture him in some way to get even.

So you can see it's perfectly reasonable that I was unable to sleep when the Saint traveled. There were "things" out there waiting to get me and my son. I was the last line of defense. Mother protector and all that. Bill didn't have to be scared of the dark when Dad was gone. He had me.

When Bill was small, a gun wasn't an option. We put in an electronic security system, which makes a nice beeping sound if you enter by a door and a horrid blaring alarm if you break glass or raise a window. Of course once the alarm beeped or went off, my only recourse was to shout, "Stop. I've got an axe handle!" (I thought that sounded more threatening than "Stop. I've got a big stick!")

A gun would have put more fear in the bad guys, but in Bill's formative years, we kept the gun in the locked file cabinet under "g" and the bullets under "b." As Bill grew up we had gun safety talks and got my dad, a retired law enforcement officer, to add some "fear of God" to the mix. Finally, when Bill reached his teens, we left the file cabinet unlocked when the Saint traveled.

No one thought I'd ever need the gun. Which was good because the gun was a 9mm automatic. You put a round in the chamber by putting the bullet clip in and then ratcheting back the top of the gun. That's pretty hard for my hands. I'm short and have hands that match. This whole automatic pistol thing is a lot harder than it looks. The guys in movies are 6' 2" and have really big hands. Handling the gun is like a toy to them. To me, it's like trying to learn Braille with calluses on your fingertips.

However unlikely and difficult using the gun for protection was, the concept was mildly comforting. At last I had a real chance against the bad guys. If I could get to the gun first, if the bullets weren't misfiled, if I remembered what to do and could actually do it.

Not long after the soccer incident, the Saint was out of town and I had occasion to use the gun. It was one a.m. Earlier, I'd set the alarm, closed the long hallway door going back to the bedrooms, and tilted a chair so that the back snugged under the door handle. The chair was a new piece of security technology I'd discovered. I liked it. I felt safer somehow. Safe enough that I drifted off to sleep before the usual three a.m.

Then the beeping started. OhmyGawd! Someone had opened the front door. The actual alarm wouldn't go off for two minutes, but those early warning beeps pumped as much adrenaline through me as any blaring alarm.

Being an intelligent modern woman, I calmly grabbed the portable phone, headed to the file cabinet, and dialed the number of the Saint's hotel in Miami. He was *so* pleased that I thought of calling *Miami* in my time of emergency. I wanted him to walk me through the whole gun thing. He wanted me to call 911. Since the alarm was still beeping, I thought it might be an alarm malfunction and I didn't want the police to think I was stupid.

Sensing a losing battle, the Saint got with the program and began instructions. I had the phone tucked against my shoulder so both hands were free. What I discovered is that ratcheting back the slide of the gun to chamber a round wasn't the hard part. Nope. The hard part was gently settling the hammer back into place as part of this process of getting the gun cocked, ready and on safety. You have to let the hammer down easy after you cock it. Real easy. Or the gun fires.

Have I mentioned that I have small hands? Short thumbs?

The hammer slipped.

All the poor Saint in Miami heard was, "No!" BOOM! Click. Dial tone.

I heard the boom. After that I didn't hear much of anything except inner ear ringing. I was in a long hallway. Doors shut. Trapped with the percussion of the gunshot. Once again I experienced one of those only-two-thoughts-going-through-your-head situations.

"Where are the cats?"

and

"His daddy is going to kill me."

God bless redial buttons. I hit that redial button for all I was worth. Couldn't hear a thing but I figured if I said, "Room 1343, please," enough times in a row that I'd eventually get to the Saint.

Oh, I got to the Saint in more ways than one that night. Once he discovered I was alive and well, his language was less than saintly. After finding out that the beeping was my cell phone battery asking for a charge, he was laughing so hard I thought I just might have to shoot *him* when he got home.

It wasn't until I got off the phone (after promising to call 911 in the future) that I realized my son hadn't come out of his room to check on me. He hadn't shouted to see if I was okay. Hell, probably hadn't even *woken up*. Before you people try and excuse the poor boy, keep in mind that I made the fateful shot while standing beside his bedroom door.

Even if he *had* woken up, my devoted son decided to go back to sleep, figuring Mom could handle it. This was a defining moment of motherhood for me. *Where was the legendary mother-son bond?* That special kind of caring through which growing boys think they've become men and feel the Neanderthal urge to take care of the little women in their lives?

Well, it wasn't in my house. All I had in my house was a purse that had been mortally wounded and a Sears credit card with a hole in it. Why I'd dropped my purse in the hallway next to my office door is one of life's little mysteries. A half-inch to the right and I'd have killed the damned cell phone that started the mess. A half-inch to the left and I wouldn't have had to answer pesky sales clerk questions about why there were holes in my credit cards. If I'd taken the purse into my office and shut the door, I'd never have heard the beeping in the first place, and I wouldn't have been standing there certain I'd done something fundamentally wrong in raising my son.

Life's like that a lot. Full of little decisions that change every piece of your future.

That night I put away the gun and crept back into my bed. I had a little bit of a hole in my heart too. I really had thought I could do this mother thing. That my own child would love me back and worry about me. That I'd always be necessary to his life somehow. Be something other than a pain in his butt.

After that the teenage years were some dark hugless years. Hugging Mom is not cool apparently. Those years were also when the first ripped-out-sleeves shirt appeared in his wardrobe. I took solace from the fact that my redneck was at least on the honor role and going away to college on a partial academic scholarship. I hadn't failed completely.

Complaining to my friends was out. They all had daughters. If I tried to explain my concerns they gave me a withering look and said, "At least he doesn't come through the front door wailing that his life is over and fling himself on his bed in a fit of hysterics. You can actually use your own telephone. And your clothes don't keep disappearing. Shut up and count your blessings."

It wasn't until he was home for the summer that first year of college that light began shining at the end of the tunnel. He had a summer job. I knew asking about his college life, girlfriends and financial situation was off limits. But I thought maybe—just maybe—we can talk about the new job. I bounded through the front door that evening hoping to catch him before he was off to visit friends.

The house was empty. Disappointment began to creep over me until I noticed the handwritten note taped to my computer screen.

Mom,

Work was good.

Gone Out. Be home probably late. You don't have to wait up. The beeping you hear will be me. Do me a favor. Try not to shoot me.

Love you,

Bill

I still have the note. It's as special as any Mother's Day card could ever be. And I'm more delighted than I would ever have thought possible to be the mom of a 3/5 redneck.

Melanie better watch out because this Scarlett is going to do a helluva job as a grandmother.

The Vinegar Files

by Linda Holmes

The four seasons are salt, pepper, mustard and vinegar.
—Kids Say the Darndest Things

Most Southern women know how to get extended, creative mileage out of any given product. For example, both of my grandmothers and Mama could find an infinite number of ways to use a paper bag during the course of its lifetime: shelf liner, lunch sack, school project, liquid blotter, or dress pattern, just to name a few. Likewise, I watched these women working in our Georgia homes over the years as they found more uses for vinegar than I could shake a stick at. As a product of this training, I ventured into creative uses of vinegar in ways that even Mama and my grandmothers didn't consider, particularly during one summer in the mid 1960's when I was 12 years old.

That was the summer that I was planning to go to camp for two weeks in August right before Labor Day weekend and getting back into school. Being an only child, Mama let me invite Trina, a girlfriend of mine from our suburban neighborhood, to go along with me to camp. We completed our camp applications together right after we got out of school for the summer, and we were thrilled near the end of June when we got our letters stating that our applications had been received and accepted.

The two of us spent a great part of our summer weeks together planning for our camp adventures, including taking swimming lessons for eight weeks at our neighborhood swimming pool. That way, we figured we would be able to at least tread water and float well enough to avoid being placed in the "beginners" level for swimming at camp. Nobody wanted to be called a "baby" when swimming hour came around.

At home, Mama's first run of cucumbers and tomatoes had just ripened in her small backyard garden, so our kitchen reeked of vinegar and pickling spices for weeks as she prepared and "put up" jar after jar of Daddy's favorite sweet pickles. We enjoyed fresh tomato sandwiches daily while the pickling was going on. The juice from the ripe tomatoes in my sandwiches always seemed to drizzle down on my shirts as I ate, and I noticed that Mama somehow got the tomato stains out every time. I was curious about this accomplishment, so I asked her about it.

"Mama, didn't this shirt have that big tomato stain on it the other day"?

"Yes ma'am, Sarah Fay, it did, but I do know something about getting stains out."

"Well, how did you do it?"

"It's simple. I just rubbed a bit of vinegar through the stain before laundering the shirt. Vinegar works on the tomato juice that way."

"Mama, is there anything that vinegar can't do?"

"I've heard that it won't draw as many flies as honey, but maybe that's about it."

Mama knew everything, or so it seemed to me at the age of twelve. While she worked on the pickles, she made one or two vinegar pies. I always wondered why the vinegar pie tasted sweet instead of sour or bitter.

"Mama, why do you call this pie a 'vinegar pie'? I inquired. "It doesn't even taste sour or strong like vinegar."

"Well, Sarah, that's part of the attraction for tasting it, you see. What you call the pie, the name of it, can either make people want to try it or make them have a big time discussing why they won't try it. Some folks will taste a "vinegar pie" just to find out if it tastes like vinegar or not."

"Does it really have vinegar in it, Mama?"

"Yes, but only a couple of teaspoonfuls to offset the sugar and vanilla's sweetness a bit. The vinegar makes the taste 'just right.'"

It was during the weeks of summer swimming lessons that circumstances led to my own first set of creative vinegar adventures. Mama and Trina's mom took turns driving us to our weekly swimming lessons. The week of the third lesson was especially hot and sultry with temperatures all the way up into the high '80's, and the humidity made us feel as sticky as ice cream when it melts on your hands and fingers. Trina and I both came home all sunburned. Back in those days, we didn't have the multitude of sun block products on the market that one finds nowadays. Instead, we had QT and zinc oxide or baby oil.

We vowed that we would have to wear a hat and a T-shirt over our swimsuits for the next weeks' lessons so we wouldn't keep on getting too much sun. When I got home, Mama took one look at me and immediately went into action.

"Goodness gracious, Sarah, you are as red as a beet. Thank goodness I know just what to do."

As I looked into the mirror in my room, I saw what Mama meant. I looked more like a lobster than a person. Mama appeared at the doorway a minute or two later with a big, wide bowl full of something that smelled pretty strong. I recognized that scent as the same one we had been smelling from the kitchen during pickling time as she began patting down my sunburned arms, legs, and face with her vinegar and water mixture.

"Now this will burn at first, but then the vinegar will take that sunburn sting right on out, and you'll be feeling better in a little bit."

Surprisingly, Mama was right. Although my skin felt like it was on fire for a few seconds, the sting dissipated quickly, and I did feel cooler and better, too after a few minutes. As I changed into play clothes and ran outside, I heard Mama telling me to be ready to ride with her to the fabric store in a half-hour.

I met up with Trina at her house, and we sat down on her front steps together.

"Whew, Sarah, what is that smell? I sure didn't smell that before you got here just now."

"Mama patted some vinegar over my sunburn. I guess you can smell it pretty strong, huh?"

"Pretty strong? I could probably smell you all the way over into the next county right now."

"We're about to ride up to the store so Mama can buy the fabric material for our camp talent night costumes," I added.

"Do you think I can have a blue outfit, and you can have the same design in another color, cause blue is my favorite?" Trina asked.

"Sure, I want pink or red, and I'll ask Mama to get blue for you." I replied.

Right then, I heard Mama calling me to come on and get in the car, so I told Trina goodbye and went on with Mama to the store. Mama could sew anything at all after she saw a picture of the desired garment; that was one of her talents.

Trina and I had drawn out a rough picture of the costumes we wanted, with sleek, long sleeves and gathered skirts; the blouses would be pastels and the skirts would be plaid or prints of some kind with the same matching background color as in the skirts' fabric. After studying our sketches, Mama cut out patterns from some paper bags and newspapers she'd saved and sized them up on us both; the next step would be getting the fabric.

Trina and I intended to win the talent competition at camp or know the reason why not, and our special costumes would help us along in that endeavor. We planned to sing one of that year's wildly popular songs that we'd heard on our transistor radios, *Turn, Turn, Turn*, by the Byrds, with lyrics from the Bible (Ecclesiastes, Chapter 3). The Vietnam War was ongoing, influencing the songs that folks remembered and shared.

Mama agreed to help us with the costumes when she heard the song and knew it carried along a Bible message for all times. She said we could be God's ambassadors at camp that way.

We arrived at the small fabric shop and got out of the car to go inside. Mama and I had just been inside the store a minute or two when several shoppers nearby looked over at us and made grimacing faces. Mama ignored them and went on about searching for the fabric that she thought would make great costumes for us. Pretty soon, I was standing alone on one side of the little shop while everyone else hovered around the store manager talking in hushed voices.

A few minutes later, I ended up having to wait in the car because of my vinegar treatment. The odor was apparently stronger than Mama or I realized. This experience came in handy the following week when Trina and I needed to think of a solution to a problem she was having with her teenaged sister.

Trina's sister was dating, and she seemed to want to flaunt this accomplishment in front of Trina and the rest of us neighborhood children who were still pre-teens. She would pick on Trina, calling her names and teasing her all the time, saying, "I get to go out on dates whenever I want to cause I'm sixteen now, and you're too young to date."

Although neither Trina nor any of the rest of us younger children cared about that dating thing (we had too many other adventures going on), it really bothered Trina that her sister wouldn't hush. The day came during July of that summer when Trina decided to take action, and she needed me to be her accomplice because of my vinegar knowledge.

"Sarah, what kind of vinegar does your Mama use on you for sunburn? You know, the stuff that smells so loud people don't want to be near you"?

"Well, we have different kinds, the regular vinegar and then some cider vinegar. Also, Mama has some vinegar that she flavors with seasonings in it and it tastes better than the regular, unseasoned kind. It may smell bad, but it sure does make a sunburn feel better if you can get through the stinging time without passing out."

"Let's go see if we can find some of the regular or cider vinegar in our kitchen. I have an idea how I can teach my smarty pants sister a lesson, if you'll help me." Trina replied.

We moved into Trina's kitchen while her Mama was outside taking in the laundry off the clothesline, and we managed to pour a good bit of vinegar into a coffee cup and make it back to Trina's room before her Mama came back into the house. Since the older sister was gone to a friend's house that day, we were able to rummage through her things without getting reprimanded, as long as we were quiet and careful. We found a cologne bottle on the dresser: bingo.

We locked ourselves in the bathroom and poured most of

the vinegar into the bottle, and then we shook it up real hard so the vinegar mixed in with the cologne. When we tested our concoction by spraying some of it on our hands, we nearly fell over due to the scent. It was perfectly odorific, just the way we wanted it. We washed our hands with soapy water before sneaking back into her sister's room and placing the cologne bottle back in its place on the dresser. That way, we wouldn't leave a vinegar-scented trail through the house.

It wasn't but an hour or so after I got back to my house that evening that Trina came running over asking if I could come outside to play for a few minutes before supper. Mama let me go out with her, and she broke down laughing as soon as we were in the yard, out of earshot.

"O.K." Trina began. "My sister has a date tomorrow night, so let's ask if you can come over tomorrow afternoon and stay the night so we can find out how she feels when somebody gets a joke on her. She'll be sure to spray on some cologne because she always does that when she's getting ready to go out on a date. I've watched her."

"I bet we get in trouble for it all," I replied.

"Well, she deserves it." Trina continued. "I'll say it was my idea if we get found out."

Mama agreed that I could spend the next evening at Trina's house. She and Daddy always thought an only child like me needed to be socialized as much as possible, so they were pleased to let me stay over at my close friends' homes occasionally.

When Trina's sister came out to greet her date, we heard her dress swishing on down the hallway toward the front door. We followed her and peeked out at the scene from a safe distance; we could both smell the vinegar odor in the air, too, so we knew the cologne had been put into action. We watched and listened as the date asked her whether she had on a new perfume and stepped back away from her as they walked out to his car.

We couldn't help ourselves as we doubled over in laughter for several minutes. Trina's Mom even asked us whether we were all right.

The next morning Trina and I scuffed into her kitchen in our pajamas and bedroom slippers for some cereal and toast, and we could hear her sister sobbing over the telephone to a girlfriend that her date didn't seem to want to be around her very long because he brought her home early. We also overheard her saying that she wondered whether her cologne was too strong.

We barely got through eating our breakfast without cracking up right then and there. The plan worked even better than we had hoped it would. We never did get "found out," at least as far as we knew. Trina's sister poured out that cologne, vowing to find a different kind that wasn't so strong, and she stopped picking on Trina so much, too. She even played "Life" or "Monopoly" with us occasionally after that experience.

I decided that the song from the Bible was right according to a twelve year-old's experiences: "To every thing there is a season and a time to every purpose under the heaven" (Ecclesiastes 1:1).

Just a couple of weeks after the cologne vinegar episode, one of the families in our neighborhood discovered that they had planted too many cucumber seeds in their backyard vegetable garden. I'm talking so many cucumbers that they even kept boxes of cucumbers in their front door hallway all the rest of the summer. When anyone stopped by their house and rang the bell, he or she received a box of cucumbers as a gift.

Everyone on the whole street grew sick of cucumbers. The Mothers in every household got out their pickle recipes, and the neighborhood grocery stores ran out of vinegar completely and had to reorder. Pickles couldn't be made fast enough because the supply was so much greater than the demand.

Finally, one of the mothers found a "cold set" recipe where the pickling juices and vinegar could all be used cold instead of having to boil everything. She helped the surplus cucumber family set up large containers in their basement as they made pickles by the barrel, instead of by the jar. We all sent our cucumbers to them at that point of the summer. Although the resulting pickles tasted pretty good, people just get tired of pickles after a while.

Trina and I were relieved when August rolled around and out parents drove us to camp for two weeks. We met the other girls in our cabin, and we ended up having a great time. Since we'd taken swimming lessons, we both got into the "intermediate" swimming section (thank goodness) instead of the "beginners" section. In the late afternoon, the girls from our cabin used our free time to practice rowing a canoe around the lake and singing at the top of our lungs.

Trina and I were a big hit on the talent night, too, and we ended up winning first place. We had practiced together all summer, and our a cappella rendition of *Turn, Turn, Turn* wasn't half bad. I'm certain that our fancy costumes helped us, too. We both got a blue ribbon, and the camp director asked us to sing again during the Sunday church meeting in the outside pavilion. Some girls from another cabin weren't too happy that their cheerleading performance with uniforms and pom-poms from their school didn't win them first place. I decided that the judges were impressed that a pop song could reflect a Bible lesson, and that Trina and I could sing it through without getting all those lyrics mixed up.

One afternoon after the talent competition, our group of campers came back to the cabin after canoeing for an hour back and forth around the lake to find that all the beds had been short-sheeted, and the toilets had been greased with Vaseline (as we discovered when we tried to sit on them and slid off onto the floor). Trina and I decided that the unhappy cheerleader campers who lost the talent competition probably did it, so the next afternoon we all hid behind some trees a distance from our cabin during free time and kept a lookout.

Sure enough, the culprits showed themselves and sprinted into our cabin while they thought we were gone canoeing.

"Let's run in there and catch them red-handed," one camper demanded.

"Yeah, she's right. Let's get 'em." another girl piped in.

"Wait a minute." I cautioned. "I have a better idea, and Trina, I bet you know what I'm thinking."

"The vinegar. Did you bring some along with you to camp, Sarah"? Trina questioned.

"Mama let me bring a small jar of it in case I got sunburned. Why don't we try it out in their cabin tomorrow afternoon while they're all gone during free time?" I suggested.

We found some of our clothes and underwear hanging from the ceiling fans and bedposts as we entered our cabin. As we cleaned up the mess, Trina and I explained about the cologne vinegar to the rest of the girls from our cabin. They agreed that it might work here at camp, too. This time, however, we would sprinkle it all over the cheerleaders' clothes and underwear so they would be all smelly when they wore the vinegar clothes.

It was hard to keep a secret that evening, and we had to make everyone in our cabin promise not to tell the plan to anybody from another cabin. The time passed so slowly we thought the following afternoon would never arrive. We watched the cheerleader campers' cabin from a safe distance until we saw them run out of their cabin for free time. One girl from our group walked over to their cabin and knocked on the door. After no one came to answer the knock, she opened the door and scanned the cabin to make sure it was empty.

"O.K. Hurry up and get in here," she yelled in a hoarse whisper.

"I'll be lookout." Trina volunteered. "The rest of you go on and pull out their clothes so Sarah can follow with the vinegar."

We quickly ran inside, doused the clothes with vinegar, and "hid" them hanging out of the trashcans so the cheerleader campers could find them pretty easily. Then we high-tailed it off to the hiking trail for a while. That evening, we were sure we could smell whiffs of vinegar through the dining hall as we ate supper, but we never said anything to anyone, and we didn't have any more trouble in our cabin, either.

Following camp, we only had a week left before school would be starting after Labor Day weekend. The surplus cucumber family sold their house at the end of the summer and moved away right before school began. When a new family moved into the pickle house a few weeks later, the story goes that they found all those barrels standing in the basement. Not knowing what to expect, they took off the lids and passed out due to the resulting fumes from pent-up pickles and pickling juices. I don't know how they disposed of all those pickles.

As school began, I mentally closed the vinegar files in my neighborhood, at least until next summer.

A Family Treasure

by Susan Sipal

Family faces are magic mirrors. Looking at people who belong to us, we see the past, present and future.
—Gail Lumet Buckley

A long time ago in a land far, far away... well, actually the Halifax County side of Littleton, North Carolina... a man buried a pot of gold beneath the end of a rainbow.

Okay, okay...it was actually during the Civil War and he hid the money under an old stump near a spring. Well, who knows if the stump was there at the time he buried it, but it was there when my Great-Grandpa sampled a bit too much moonshine and went hunting nearby.

See according to my father, his grandfather (whom we all called Pa) claimed to have heard a ghostly voice revealing the location of this hidden treasure. And Daddy's Grandma Leah, who always did like to set her husband's tall-tales straight, never said a word contrary to *this* particular story.

You have to understand a bit of family history here. My family evolved from the apes in northeastern North Carolina. Either that or they came over on the Mayflower, went straight to Halifax-Warren Counties, and haven't moved since. Because if you trace any of my four lines back, they've all been in the region since the mid-1600s. And they're quite interrelated. In fact, on one side of the family tree, there are lots of cousins who were more than just the kissing kind.

Like any Good Southern Family, we're descended from royalty (who cares that it's five centuries ago). And we have the obligatory tale of great family wealth lost by previous generations. For ours it was the result of a lake development that passed us by.

My Myrick ancestors owned most of the land under what is now Gaston Lake. When my great-great grandfather was fixing up his will and deciding which of his twelve children to give what to, he asked each of them what parcel of his thousand acres they wanted. Pa, in his infinite wisdom, said he didn't want any of the land that bordered the Roanoke River as it flooded too dad-burn much. He'd take his up along the highway.

And so forever after Pa worked a hundred acres of prime red clay, whereas his siblings inherited land that sold for thousands when the Army Corps of Engineers bought them out to build Gaston Lake. With what they didn't sell, they used their strong business acumen to develop into lakeside resort homes.

Oh, well.

My family fortune lost before my father was even a twinkle in my grandfather's eye.

But *that* family wealth was always truly lost. We knew there was no way to recover it.

There was, however, another family treasure that tantalized me as a child, bewitching me with its possibilities. Its allure was part archaeological and part treasure hunter. For it was a buried fortune, stashed underground since Civil War times.

Once again, I reckon I ought to be like Grandma Leah and set my story straight too. It was not actually during the War Between the States that this hoard was buried—it was during Reconstruction, and it wasn't treasure, but gold and silver coins, and lots of them. Or so we'd always liked to believe.

It was rumored that an old miser who'd sharecropped land on Pa's farm (when it still belonged to his father as part of the great plantation) had buried his gold coins on Pa's property. During that uncertain era, many people in the South hid their money. No one trusted a bank, and certainly no one trusted the Yankees not to tax and steal it.

Unfortunately, the tenant farmer not only didn't trust the bank or the Yankees; he didn't trust his family either. He told no one where he buried his coins. Of course, being a sharecropper, there probably wasn't much to it, but at that time it would have been real gold and silver, not this fake stuff we have now.

After his death, it was rumored his wife and kids went crazy digging up the land, looking for his stash of wealth.

It was never found.

Or if it was, no one ever made it known.

But many years later, Pa was out hunting and chased a rabbit into a thicket. As he neared a spring, near that miser's long abandoned house, the rabbit disappeared. Pa, tired, plopped down on a stump near a spring to rest.

And that's when he heard the Voice.

"This be where I buried my gold."

Pa looked around him, but no one was about. He searched behind a tree, under a bush, and even inside a hollow log.

No one.

"This is where I buried my coins," the voice said again.

Well, not being a fool, Pa instantly noted where he was and later showed my father the site.

I ate this story up as a child, never questioning why having been told the exact location of an immense fortune, Pa didn't instantly go dig it up and live a life of wealth and privilege the rest of his days instead of barely scraping to get by. Nor my father, who did better than just scrape to get by, but certainly didn't live the life of someone who knows the whereabouts of a long buried fortune.

Perhaps the wealth did not matter to them. What mattered was knowing a treasure was out there, and having the secret key to finding it.

If one were to go look, and find nothing, perhaps one would lose that special key.

And wouldn't that be disappointing?

No, it was much better to recount the tale for a new generation, and leave the hoard exactly where it lay buried. Secure in the knowledge that only *we* knew where to find it.

Prosaically, Pa probably never bothered digging those coins up because he didn't have a shiny new metal detector like we did, or maybe he didn't want to disturb the tranquil beauty of the area, or maybe it was just that he preferred a good, rich story to tons of gold.

'Cause he was a storyteller. My father after him.

And I'm a lot like them both.

Don't matter if the story's 100% proof or not, what matters is that it's smooth going down, warms your gut, and has just a wee kernel of truth... just who knows where.

So sit back, take a load off, and let me tell you about the day Daddy, Mama, my brother, sister and I decided to find the old family treasure.

One Father's Day afternoon many (I'm not telling how many) years ago, my family set off from church in our station wagon, fake wood running down the sides, with Daddy's new gift. We kids had devised the purely unselfish idea to buy him a metal detector to finally find and dig up this fortune we'd been hearing about for years (Mama chipping in the largest contribution, of course).

And that's when the fun started, driving down state route 58 toward my great-grandparents' home place.

Mama was giving Daddy driving lessons, again. "David, slow down, don't get so near that car, can't you see?"

While my brother and I played in the backseat. "Mama, he pulled my hair."

"Did not. Besides she punched me in the stomach."

"Why do we have to go to Grandma Leah's today?" I sulked deeper in my seat. "No one's there, and I wanted to play with Katie."

Bill scrunched in the foot of the car, tying our sister's shoelaces together without her notice. "Well, I'm missing Batman on TV, then Scooby, then..."

Sharon tried her hardest to get away from us brats, squeezing into a corner of the seat, twisting her finger around her hair. "Can't you two please grow up?" she said in her oh-so-mature voice, then burrowed deeper behind her *Teen Magazine*. At thirteen, she was four years older than me, and six older than Bill.

I stuck my tongue out at her hidden face, then poked my brother again. "Butt-head," I whispered, but not low enough.

"Susan, don't call your brother names." Mama twisted in the front seat to give me *the look*. "Now you two calm down and do something fun together. We're almost there. Why don't you count cows?"

"They smell like poop."

"You can't smell them from here."

"How much longer...?" Bill let the end drawl out into a long, aggravating whine, which he'd perfected.

"Almost there." Daddy's voice was low, his jaw clenched as if he couldn't wait to arrive either. "Who'll be the first to see Grandma Leah's house?"

Bill and I perked up at that, struggling to get in the opening near the front seat (this being the days before seat belts). My sister merely sniffed and turned another page. Beneath her dignity once again.

"I see it."

"I saw it first!"

"No, you didn't."

"Yes, I did."

"But I said so first, so I win."

"Will you two shut up?" Mama yelled.

We were so used to hearing these words that we continued on. Actually, aggravating each other was our prime source of entertainment, when we were denied the company of our friends or TV, until the rare occasion when we joined forces to terrorize Sharon. Now *that* was a blast.

But unfortunately we arrived at Grandma and Pa's before we had her shrieking.

We tumbled out of the car, Bill and I each trying to be first, and ran for the farmhouse, deserted now, the windows boarded up as if she were asleep with eyes closed. Great-Grandma Leah had died a couple of years ago, Pa several years before that, and the place stood empty, lonely, as if waiting for us to come, open her up to the sun, run through the old rooms built by long ago family, and fill it once again with sunshine and laughter.

"Hey, Daddy, the door's locked," I shouted, rattling the front door, trying to force it open.

"Bill, Susan, come on. Don't mess around there." Mama waved to us from underneath the worm-eaten pecan tree. "We're heading down the path."

Daddy was pulling his new metal detector out of the back of the station wagon. "Yes, Sharon, you have to come, too. You're not sitting in the car all day listening to the radio and running down the battery like last time. We're doing this as a family. And you're going to enjoy yourself."

A shovel fell out, slamming against his foot, ending his explanation in a bad word (one which Mama threatened to wash out of my brother's mouth with soap when he repeated it a week ago). "Now get out and be quiet," he barked.

Sharon sniffed. "But Mary Jane invited me to go roller skating today. And there's a boy-girl party tonight at Brandy's. I don't understan—"

"Because I said so."

The logic that was supposed to end all arguments. Problem was, it never did.

Sharon continued to whine about the missed opportunities with her friends, her oh-so-mature and sophisticated friends, while Bill and I tore down the path like a couple of wild chimps on the loose, shrieking and carrying on, as Mama liked to say.

A bright, Carolina-blue sky blazed overhead as we raced up the dirt path skirting the peanut field (still worked by sharecroppers who nowadays lived on their own farm) toward the woods at the far end. We didn't know exactly where to go, but we knew *it* was in that general direction, and each of us determined to reach *it* first.

Treasure.

Images of a pirate's chest filled with gold and jewels, my hands burrowing deep, jewels sliding between my fingers, rushed through my imagination. I'd buy that Shaun Cassidy album I'd been wanting, along with an 8-track player, some new bell-bottom jeans—

"I get first dibs." My brother's claim burst my bubble.

"Do not!"

"*Do too.*"

"It was my idea—"

"Susan, Bill, hush." Mama shouted to us from further behind.

"We're probably not going to find anything, but what we do will have to be split equally, with your uncles as well."

"I'm keeping whatever I find," I whispered to Bill out of the corner of my mouth."

"Me too."

A glint of reflected sunlight at the side of the path caught my eye.

"Hey, look at that." I bent to dig my fingers around a pretty rock. "I think it's gold."

"Oh, you're so immature," Sharon said over my shoulder, obviously having rushed to catch up with us. "That's just a piece of *fool's* gold."

"Is not." I turned to Daddy, who panted a bit as he wrestled with the metal detector, two shovels and a rake. "Is it, Daddy?"

He took the palm-sized, shiny gold rock out of my hand, turning it over as he studied it. "Looks like mica to me."

"Mica? What's that?"

"A type of rock common in this area." He broke off a section of it, coming off in sheets. "See how it flakes. It's used a lot in electronics. Here." He passed it back to me.

I stuffed it in the pocket of my jeans. It might not be gold, but it sure was pretty. Maybe I could put it in my fish tank.

"Now, come on, kids," Daddy called. "We're heading this way."

He led us down a path that was so overgrown with weeds, it was hard to tell it was a path anymore.

"Where does this go?" Sharon asked.

"Toward the home place of that miser. Bill," he shouted, grabbing my brother's arm, stopping him before he headed into a clump of shiny leaves. "That's poison ivy."

"Poison what? How can you tell? I wanted to add some to my leaf collection."

Daddy explained how to tell poison ivy, then showed us some poison oak climbing up a nearby pine. I scratched myself just remembering the rash I'd had last spring after playing near the old well at Grandma's farm.

As we hiked, Daddy pointed out the differences between white oaks and red oaks, while Mama showed us where some blackberry bushes grew.

"Now, don't pick the red ones," she said. "The black ones are ripe."

I'd already figured that out, my mouth crammed with the tart, seedy fruit. Bill had blackberry juice running down his chin. I laughed at him.

"Just a bit further." Daddy directed us down the path.

Even Sharon had stopped complaining. True, she wasn't chomping on blackberries like me and Bill, turning her nose up at what birds had obviously pooped on, but she had quite a nice collection of wildflowers in her hand.

"You know what Mama said these are called?" she asked me, shoving some yellow flowers with a black center in my face. They didn't smell very good.

"No." I elbowed her away.

"Black-eyed Susans." She smirked. "Which is exactly what you'll be next time I catch you reading my diary."

"I told you, I didn't—"

"Sharon, Susan." Mama's tone stopped us both. Sounded like she was about at her "don't tread on me" edge.

"Here we are." Daddy led us behind the crumbling farmhouse to where a small creek bubbled out of the ground beneath a nearby boulder. "Now this," Daddy paused for dramatic effect, "is where Pa told me he heard the voice. So, if there's any gold to be found, it should be within a few yards of here."

"I want to use it first." Three voices clamored as one, with three pairs of hands all reaching for the new metal detector.

"*I'll* use the metal detector until we know how it works," Daddy stopped the erupting argument, "then we'll go down by age. First Sharon, then Susan and Bill."

"Why am I always last?" Bill stomped his foot.

"Because we save the best for last." Mama gave him a sideways hug.

"Do not," I muttered for only him to hear. "Because you're the baby and always will be—"

"Susan!"

"Yes, ma'am," I grumbled.

"Now, Sharon, you take this rake, and Bill and Susan you use these shovels to dig up whatever we find." Daddy passed out the tools, once again thwarting an argument before it got going good.

With something to occupy our hands, we followed along behind Daddy, eagerly listening to the beeps for a special sound to occur. We were so quiet in our anticipation; we could hear our own excited breathing.

"Look," Mama whispered. "Over there."

All three gazes followed Mama's pointed finger. A beautiful deer, a doe obviously, her fawn by her side, watched us warily—her long neck twisted, her large brown eyes widened, her ears pricked far back on her head, her skinny legs bent in preparation to flee.

We all held our breaths.

"Can I pet the baby?" Bill asked in a seven-year-old loud whisper.

Hooves crashing through the dry leaves, the doe and her fawn fled, a flock of black crows swooshing into flight from the tall oak nearby, their caws protesting the upset.

"Well, no one can pet it now," Sharon said.

"Thanks, Bill," I added, but without much heat. I'd been excited too.

"I didn't mean—"

"It's okay." Daddy calmed us. "Listen."

The metal detector beeped at a higher pitch. Our whoops matched its noise.

"Let me dig first."

"No, me."

Mama took charge. "Here, Sharon, you rake the leaves back from this area, and Susan you dig over here and Bill you over there."

Within minutes we had uncovered a rusty, metal...I didn't know what, it was so caked with mud.

"That's a horseshoe," Daddy said.

Bill laughed. "I didn't know horses wore shoes."

"Well, you haven't been around them much, but when horses work hard, their hooves get sore and wear out. So farmers put these metal buffers on them for protection." Daddy dug clumps of dirt out of the crevices, his eyes crinkled in the corners with amusement. "You know, they used not to have tractors and cars. The horses provided that labor, and the farmers had to protect their livestock if they wanted to eat."

"Cool." Bill's blue eyes widened. "Can I have it?"

Neither Sharon nor I had any interest in the dirty old thing, so Bill jammed one end in his back pocket.

We scoured the area for what seemed like hours, finding rusting bits of farm implements, soda-drink bottle tops, and even an Indian-head nickel and a wheat-shaft penny. Daddy and Mama shared stories with each new find—about growing up on a farm, and the hard work they'd done even at our age, priming tobacco, picking cotton. Mama told how she and her brothers had jumped in the soft piles of cotton until Grandma threatened to tan their hides. Daddy spent his hard-earned money on Grape Nehis and serial matinees. And they'd both bought soda drinks for a nickel at the local counter-drugstore. Instead of skating rinks, TV, and malls, they'd spent the long hot summers playing in these woods (or for Mama, those near her home) with cousins and the tenant farmers' children.

We found a turtle shell, soft green moss, and more worms than I could count.

But no treasure.

Once I startled a mother rabbit and her five little bunnies from their den, but they all hopped away before Bill and I could catch one. And we all constantly slapped at the mosquitoes. But at least no snakes.

And no treasure.

Then it started raining, a typical late-afternoon summer thunderstorm, and we rushed for Grandma Leah's house, frustrated, mud splattering the bottom of our pant-legs.

Mama made us empty our pockets on the back porch. I had several more pretty rocks, including a real quartz, some pieces of antique pottery, and the best find—a handful of old glass marbles. Bill's pockets were so stinky with blackberry juice from the berries he'd stuffed in them and squished worm guts that Mama made him change clothes and put on the extra pair of shorts she'd brought just in case. Sharon, meanwhile, had nothing in her pockets but clutched a fistful of Black-eyed Susans and Queen Anne's lace.

While Mama helped me pull beggar lice and hitchhikers off my pants, Sharon and Daddy found an old milk bottle out in the dilapidated barn, which they filled with water at the well. Then Mama forced us to wash the red mud from our shoes and hands before she'd let us in the car.

Against our protests to outwait the rain and try again, Mama and Daddy herded us in the station wagon, storing our treasures in the back.

"I think I found the best thing," Bill said.

"What was that?" I asked.

"The horseshoe."

"Yeah, that was pretty cool." I shared one of my marbles with him. "But I like my marbles better."

"You know, Susan." Sharon took the other one, studying it. "I've heard these are quite collectible. You ought to take good care of them." She passed it back to me.

"Are you kids tired?" Mama asked from the front seat, yawning.

"Not me." Bill bundled his dirty jeans into a pillow against the window.

I lent him my jacket to use as well. "I wish it hadn't started raining."

"Yeah, me too." Sharon flipped her magazine over in her lap as a desk for examining the few coins we'd found. "When can we go again?"

Rain splattered harder outside, fogging our windows and cocooning us within, as we made plans for returning. We couldn't go the next weekend because of Sharon's piano recital. Then Bill had a T-ball tournament the following Saturday, and summer Vacation Bible School started the week after that. But we set a definite date for a weekend in late July.

"I can't wait," we all three chimed together.

We hadn't found the fortune. It remained pure, untouched, a dream still worth dreaming. Perhaps we'd search for it again someday, but mostly we'd cherish it in our minds, a kind of exciting assurance that there was a family treasure always lurking just a bit beyond our reach, and yet sometimes, completely within our grasp.

For one fine Father's Day, we'd actually found the family wealth buried within our hearts.

A Sunday Dress

by Betty Cordell

The gem cannot be polished without friction, not a man perfected without trials.
—Chinese Proverb

I came home from school that day and charged back to my bedroom, eager to shed the hated dress I had to wear to school and get into my comfortable jeans. It was totally unfair that boys got to wear jeans while we girls were stuck with skirts. How could you hang upside down on a jungle gym in a skirt? Dumb! I threw my books on the desk, tore off my sweater, and wriggled out of the dress, stomping on it for good measure after it dropped to the floor. Catching myself, I checked quickly behind me to make sure Mama hadn't caught me in my show of temperament. Nice Southern girls didn't stomp their clothes.

It was 1958 and I was in fourth grade. I had waited all day for the time when I could finally pull on my jeans and veg out. I already knew which ones I wanted to wear. I had only one pair I'd worn enough and put through the washer the right number of times to be sufficiently soft and faded to perfection.

Eagerly, I jerked open the closet door and flipped through the jeans and slacks hanging there. No luck. I pawed through them again and stared in disbelief. My favorite pair of jeans wasn't there. Another pair was missing, too. I was supposed to have four pairs of jeans in various "break-in" states, but only two pairs hung in my closet. I ran to the bathroom and rummaged through the hamper. Not there. I grabbed my robe and hurried to the laundry room. Not there, either. Puzzled, but suspicious, I went back to my room and began a diligent search through the rest of my clothes. My suspicions were confirmed. To my horror, in addition to the two pair of jeans, three shirts—including the new one with the navy pinstripes—some underwear, my royal-blue mohair cardigan that had brass buttons stamped with a design like a knight's coat of arms that I'd been given last Christmas by Aunt Ruby, and my pink nightgown with the white lace trim were all missing.

I knew exactly what had happened. My mother had struck again.

"Mo-o-o-ther!" I yelled.

In a moment she appeared at my door, a look of annoyance on her face. "What in the world are you yelling about?"

"Where are all my clothes?" I asked in my most plaintive voice, knowing what the answer would be.

The look of annoyance vanished and the concerned look I knew so well spread across her face. "Well, honey," she said, "something really terrible happened last night to a family on the other side of town. Their home burned down and they lost everything. They have a daughter about your age and I knew you'd want to help out by giving some of your clothes to her."

I ignored the stab of guilt I felt and convinced myself that my feelings were totally justified. Being careful not to cross the line into disrespect, which might have merited a trip to the switch bush—even at my age—I continued my whine.

"But, Mama, couldn't you have given her some of my old stuff? You know, the things I don't like anymore? And why did you give her my pretty pink nightgown? It was my favorite. *And* my royal blue sweater! I loved that sweater."

After gazing a minute at my distressed face, my mother said in her 'no nonsense' voice, "Get in the car. I'm taking you somewhere."

"Where?" I asked.

"Just get in the car," she said, picking up her purse and heading for the door.

I knew Mama was irritated with me, so I didn't chance any more questions. She started the car, and we drove down our street to the corner and turned. When we got to Bellevue we continued across until we got to the main road on the other side of town. We crossed that road and continued into a neighborhood I'd never seen before.

The houses were small and didn't have much grass in the front yards. Kids of all ages were playing ball in the street and had to move out of the way for our car to pass. The paint was peeling off the wood siding on the houses along the street, and gaping holes were torn through the screen doors. Broken windows had newspapers stuffed through the cracked glass. Old rusted cars sat in the driveways, and a few men leaned against them talking. The whole atmosphere made me feel uncomfortable and a little afraid. Even the pavement on the streets was full of potholes that my mother mostly dodged, but occasionally bumped through, as she guided the car down the street. But my mother drove on like she was completely familiar with this area.

"Mama," I said, "I don't like this place. Where are we?"

"This is where most of the workers at the woolen mill live. The mill had to lay off about a third of their employees a few months ago and the people here are having a really hard time—some, more than most. Like the family that lost their home last night. Our church has been collecting food to give to these families since the layoffs."

She pulled to one side and stopped. "Look," she said.

I gazed out the window. Charred remains were all that was left of what had once been a house just like a dozen others on the street—shotgun houses, they called them. Four rooms with a center hallway. A blackened refrigerator rose just above the rubble and tilted at a crazy angle. Pieces of screens lay in the ashes on the ground. A dented water heater still stood where the back porch had been.

"A little girl just a year younger than you are," Mama said, "was awakened out of a sound sleep last night and pulled out of her house in only a pair of pajamas. Her name is Lizzie. Last night, she didn't have time to pick up her favorite stuffed animal, or put on a pair of jeans, or even a pair of shoes. I'm told the fire spread very fast. She and her family stayed in the shelter downtown last night. This is all that's left of their home."

I began to feel sick inside—the way you feel when you suddenly lose your appetite, but with a heavy load of guilt and a twinge of embarrassment thrown in for good measure.

My mother continued, "Lizzie didn't have much to begin with. Her father has been out of work and drawing government assistance for several months. But this morning, she had no shoes, no shirts, no jeans, and no home to live in. Think how you would feel if you had nothing of your own—not even your own bed to sleep in."

I stared at my hands in my lap. I didn't like to think about bad things. And I didn't like for Mama to think I wasn't a good person.

Mama's voice had a catch in it when she said, "Your pretty clothes made Lizzie smile today, and she doesn't have much to smile about. Do you understand now why I gave your clothes to her?"

I tried to imagine coming home from school and finding ashes where our house had been and never seeing my room again. Tears rolled down my cheeks. I nodded my head. "Yes, Mama, I'm sorry I didn't want Lizzie to have my clothes. Maybe I can find a book or a toy to give to her, too."

Mama gave me a big hug. "That's my girl."

In time, I came to accept that when people in our town fell on tough times, we always helped out and always with our *best* things. I'm no angel. I suffered an occasional pang when I gave up a particularly pretty sweater or dress or coat I really liked, but it was easier to do when I imagined myself in the place of those girls who were my age and had lost so much. At my worst, I must admit I prayed for God to only let families with boys have troubles or at least to not let them live in Dublin, Georgia.

Dublin is a little town in central Georgia that was founded by a man whose wife was from Ireland. He doted on his young, homesick wife and named the town Dublin to please her. Every year, the whole town came together to celebrate St. Patrick's with a Miss St. Patrick's Festival contest, a pancake breakfast, a community sing, a talent show, a crafts fair, and a parade. We had a real sense of community in Dublin with neighbors helping neighbors as the need arose, and my mother was always among the first to respond.

I found myself remembering the Lizzie story when, a few years after my father died, I escorted my still-beautiful-but-aging mother to her sixtieth class reunion at Ware County High School, just outside of Waycross, Georgia. My mother's excitement had been growing for some time. Because of her own and her friends' health issues, as well as difficulties in traveling, she hadn't seen her best friends from childhood in several years. From Dublin, she planned a luncheon to give for the twelve members of her class who would be attending the reunion. It was scheduled to be held at the Holiday Inn, where we were staying, on the day following the official reception. I was recruited to address envelopes for the invitations and consulted concerning flower arrangements and the food to be served.

The reception was held in April on the grounds of the old high school, now converted to an elementary school. The weather was beautiful—moderately warm with brilliant sunshine. In South Georgia, the forsythia and azaleas were already in bloom, and dogwoods filled with white blossoms dotted the woods along the side of the road. The organizers had set up picnic tables under a canopy of live oak trees and the boards strained under a tantalizing spread of potato salad, coleslaw, marinated bean salad, squash casserole, black eyed peas, creamed corn, butterbeans, sliced ham, fried chicken, barbecued short ribs, rolls, cornbread, peach cobbler, and several jugs of sweet tea. A crowd hovered over the tables filling their paper plates and talking when we drove up.

As I looked around, I saw that the alumni were all accompanied by members of their families who elected to stand to the side and watch the touching reunions between classmates. Some of the classmates, I learned later, had not seen each other in the sixty years since they'd graduated. The scene was made more poignant to me by the certain knowledge that few in this aged group would have another opportunity to see each other again after this reunion.

As I was helping Mother from the car, we heard an enthusiastic shout of "Lenora!" I looked up to see a tall slim woman striding toward us.

"Nancy!" Mother called out and the two were soon hugging and telling each other how wonderful they looked.

Several mobility-challenged elderly women, leaning on a variety of walking sticks for support, descended on us at once, calling out: "Lenora!" "There's Lenora!" They smothered my mother in hugs and acknowledged her introductions of me with a nod and a pat on the arm. The gaggle of voices overlapped as they began to catch up with each other.

Myrtle, a rouged and powdered, blue-haired classmate to whom I'd just been introduced, took me aside for a play-by-play of the crowd that had gathered around my mother.

"That's Nancy," she said, pointing. "She was our star basketball player. She went on to the University of Georgia, but I don't think she played basketball there. She's a scratch golfer. Beats all the men she plays with. 'Course, they're a bunch of pansies. Every little ache and pain stops them cold. Those of us who've had babies aren't bothered by the little aches and pains, are we, dear? You do have children, don't you, honey?" She searched my eyes for confirmation she hadn't just made a faux pas.

"Yes, ma'am, I do," I said.

She broke out in a big smile and said, "Why certainly you do. What do you have, darling?"

"I have a girl, age twelve, and a boy, age eighteen."

"Why, honey, you don't look old enough to have children that age."

She squeezed my hand and went on with her recital. "And you know Nelda, don't you? Your mother lived with her after she ran away from the farm. Nelda was always the class clown. Look at her! She's still at it. Bless her heart, she wouldn't understand decorum if it rose up and slapped her in the face."

I looked and, sure enough, Nelda was making goofy faces—at age seventy-eight!

"Nelda was always getting into trouble, you know. Made the teacher spray ink all over herself one time when Nelda substituted ink for the teacher's cologne. Miss Krebs used to spray herself several times a day. Said it helped diffuse the odor her students exuded after they'd spent time on the playground. She was a bit la-di-da, you know.

"Now, Doris—you know Doris, don't you, honey? Nelda's older sister?"

"Yes, ma'am," I said. I knew all the Casons. They'd let my mother live with them and finish high school after my grandfather decided that education was wasted on girls and that he needed her to work full time on the farm.

"Doris was the serious one. Class president and organizer of every event we had at school. Her parents made her wait to start school 'cause she was a winter baby. So she and Nelda ended up in the same class."

She went on. "'Course, you know what we always called Lenora, don't you?"

I shook my head. "No, ma'am, I don't."

"Lenora was always the pretty one. If we wanted a boy to talk to us, we'd go stand by Lenora. Sooner or later some boys would come over."

I laughed but found it difficult to adjust to my mother being called Lenora. When she and my father first began to date, he, being a North Georgia farm boy, found it difficult to wrap his mouth around the name "Lenora." Since mother's maiden name was McCook, Daddy took to calling her "Cookie" and it stuck. That was all I'd ever heard her called in Dublin.

The reception for the 1928 Purple Martins was pretty jovial, considering the major topic of conversation, as far as I could tell, was who had died. The organizers handed out gold T-shirts with purple martins and *Ware County High School* on them. And these elderly women—none of the few remaining men were well enough to attend—pulled the shirts on over their permed and set hairdos and soft, lumpy bodies.

Even my fashion-conscious mother! They lined up with their arms around each other and shouted out a purple martin school cheer. How they remembered it after sixty years was a mystery to me. This was just the kind of scene Charles Kuralt would have loved for his *On the Road* program.

I had never before heard of purple martins being the name of a team or a school mascot, but it somehow fit these women. Purple martins were considered important birds in South Georgia before air conditioning, when windows had to be left open at night during the summer. Back then, people strung rows of gourds in their backyards to entice the large, iridescent, bluish-black birds to come nest there because purple martins are said to eat their weight in mosquitoes and other flying insects every day.

The reception lasted less than three hours. By that time, the honorees were tired. Most lived within easy driving distance and planned to return the next day for the luncheon my mother had planned.

When we were walking back to the car, Mother pointed out a woman walking ahead of us. "That's Sally Leonard," she said in a low voice. "She was the rich girl in our class. Her family had money year round because they had pine trees."

"Pine trees?" I asked, "What do you mean?"

"The rest of us just had farm land. We only had an income during the growing season. But Sally's family had both a farm and pine trees. In the winter, her family tapped the trees for sap and sold it to be made into pitch and turpentine. Sally had a special dress for church on Sundays." Her voice was wistful.

I was stunned into silence by the thought of the little girl of sixty-odd years ago still longing for that special dress to wear on Sundays. I'd never realized. I'd never thought about what it meant to grow up "poor." I'd always had so much; I'd taken it for granted that everyone wore nice clothes to church on Sundays. I thought of those little girls who had ended up with some of my favorite clothes when I was growing up. At the moment, I couldn't remember if Mother had ever given away any of my "Sunday" dresses. I hoped so.

Back at the Holiday Inn after Mother had napped, we checked on the arrangements for the next day's luncheon. As we worked, I could see more and more how important it was to her for everything to be perfect. Her schoolmates had known her as the daughter of a hardscrabble farmer, pulling a tobacco living out of sandy soil far off the main road. Her mother had died in the Spanish flu epidemic when she was seven, and her father had married her mother's sister out of practical necessity. The sister's husband had abandoned her and her five children, and she needed a man's support. My grandfather needed a woman to run his household and care for his children. Mother was the oldest and, consequently, always had to work hard—so hard, her young damaged joints provided fertile ground for arthritis to settle in as she aged.

I looked at the hands distributing the place cards on the U shaped table. The knuckles were swollen and gnarled. At an age when I had taken dance and piano lessons after school, my mother had spent her afternoons pulling tobacco leaves and hefting them on heavy sticks up into the curing barn to dry. Fortunately, my father had earned a good living, and I felt like my mother relished this opportunity to show her classmates how far she'd come from that dirt-poor little girl without a Sunday dress.

The next day, my mother's classmates arrived promptly at twelve, a few with husbands in tow. The smell of the multiple colognes was overpowering until the roast beef, vegetables, salad, and rolls were brought in to challenge it. The stories began again—not just from Myrtle, but from the others as well, some of whom took issue with Myrtle's versions.

With several contributing her own version of each story, I learned that Nancy had played half a basketball game with her uniform pants ripped all the way up her backside. Myrtle had been the first to try make-up in their class—with disastrous results, which the teacher had made her wash off. In my opinion, the teacher was still needed. When it came to make-up, Myrtle seemed to think more was better. My mother had attracted a boy who was so smitten with her that her friends had taken to calling him "the shadow." Everywhere they went, he was sure to be nearby.

Most of the stories were told on Nelda. I heard the ink story and a hooky story (she got caught) and a story about how she shaved her legs and tried to hide the fact from her mother by letting down the hems of her dresses and claiming she'd shrunk.

As my mother and her friends told their stories, they occasionally made references to things that only they knew about. They would say code words and laugh. It was a treat to see how my mother interacted with her schoolmates. These women didn't seem elderly at all. They were funny, intelligent, charming, and appealing. I watched in amazement as a personality I'd never experienced in our household emerged from my mother. This Lenora was coquettish, a teaser, someone who reminded her friends of past faux pas, and poked them in the ribs for emphasis. I saw the girl my mother had been sixty years ago and wished I could have known her then and been one of her friends.

The luncheon was over too soon. After lengthy good-byes and checking out of the motel, we drove around to all the places Mother wanted to see before going back to Dublin. We went past a friend's pink Victorian house, gussied up with white wooden lacework along the porch and the gables. We drove over a creek where Mother told me she'd been baptized when she was twelve. And we went past the house where Mother had cooked and cleaned house after school to pay her expenses after she ran away. But she didn't mention going by one place.

"Mother, aren't we going to go by the farm?" I asked.

She looked at me and then stared straight ahead. "I'd just as soon forget it. I don't have any good childhood memories. When I lived there," she said, "we barely had enough to keep us all fed and clothed. Actually, we didn't keep ourselves clothed. The ladies from the churches in town did that. They'd come out to the farm with paper bags full of old clothes for us, and we'd pick through them and try to find the closest sizes to what we were. I hardly ever found shoes to fit. And the clothes were never in good condition. We had to patch them and sew up seams and try to get stains out. Nobody ever gave us nice, pretty clothes to wear. I used to dream about being rich and buying new clothes in bright colors."

A light of understanding dawned on me. For the first time, I truly understood why mother had given away my good clothes—my best clothes—when I was growing up. Because of her own childhood experiences, she'd made it her mission to see that other children in unfortunate circumstances never had to wear old patched and stained clothes like she had.

I didn't say anything more and kept driving. Just before I got to the junction that would have put us on the main road out of town, she said, "Well, maybe we could just drive down the road and see if it's still there. It's probably fallen down by now."

She directed me down another road that made a loop through palmetto-studded pine forests and began looking for the turnoff. We finally spotted a graveled road in the right place and turned onto it. I could sense the tension in my mother increase the closer we got to the place where she'd spent such a hard childhood. A half-mile down the road, we spotted it.

I had memories of the farm from when I was a little girl, but it never looked like this. The house was painted a pretty blue with white trim and green shutters and white wicker rockers lined the front porch. There was a little patch of grass in the front, and a walkway with pink vinca on either side of it led to the porch steps. The outbuildings, as well, seemed sturdy and well maintained—quite different from the ramshackle buildings of my memory.

With a sharp intake of breath, my mother exclaimed, "Oh, my!"

When we drove up, a woman came out. We introduced ourselves and explained who we were and why we were there. Mrs. Walters, as she introduced herself in turn, generously invited us to look around all we pleased.

"I can hardly believe my eyes," Mother said, looking at what she was seeing as if it were a banquet for her eyes. We walked to the old well and noticed it was just decorative now.

"If you only knew how many gallons of water I had to draw from this well and lug to the house or the barn!" she said, shaking her head.

She pointed to a large rock that formed an accent piece in a bed of blooming daffodils and said, "That's where I used to sit when I plucked the down off the geese for our feather beds."

"While they were alive?"

"Of course. The only time we killed a goose was at Christmas. We needed them for their eggs and their down. I'd sit with their heads caught between my legs and pluck the down from their tails."

I couldn't imagine that. Mother was telling me things today she'd never mentioned the whole time I was growing up.

We walked toward the stable where Dan, the plow horse, lived in my childhood memory. The barn was in good repair and a tractor was parked inside.

"They must be making a living here," Mother said. "I guess it's easier when you don't have ten mouths to feed."

Walking back toward the house, she pointed to a spot next to the back door. "That's where our potato hill was."

"What's a potato hill?" I asked, totally clueless.

"It's a hill made for storing sweet potatoes through the winter. We didn't have a root cellar for them. First, we dried the potatoes in the sun, then layered them with dirt and straw between each layer until we had a hill. When we wanted potatoes, we'd scrap off a layer of dirt and pull out the potatoes."

Amazing, the things I was learning!

Back at the house, Mother stopped and looked at it a long time. I could only imagine the flood of memories rushing through her mind.

"Mama," I said, "look at all you overcame to get to where you are now. They say that what doesn't kill you makes you stronger."

"Well, I must be as strong as Arnold Schwarzenegger, then," she said with a grin.

I chuckled as a vision of my mother with bulging muscles flitted through my mind. I was thrilled that her tension had faded, and it appeared she'd finally begun to gain a healthy perspective on her past.

We thanked Mrs. Walters, declining her invitation to stay for a glass of sweet tea, and got back on the road to Dublin.

After a few miles in silence, I looked over and saw a smile playing on Mother's lips.

"You know," she said, "Myrtle hasn't learned one new thing about make-up in sixty years."

I laughed. "She did overdo it a bit, didn't she?"

"And Nelda is proof that some people never change." She paused a moment, reflecting, and added, "Sometimes that's good."

Author's note: People like to talk about the "steel magnolias" of the South. Most of the time they're referring to the women who keep their men and their children under their control while letting them think all the choices they make are their own. Sometimes the expression refers to women who take over and run the family businesses after their husbands die. And sometimes it describes women like former Georgia governor Zell Miller's mother, who, after she was widowed, built a house for herself and her children with her own hands, carrying the heavy stones from a creek to the building site.

My mother was a steel magnolia, a real Southern lady. Though not all of the above story is true, my mother survived a childhood of back-breaking hard work and an unsympathetic father who was too overcome with his own responsibilities to pay attention to his children individually. She did what was necessary to get an education and a good job where she met my father. And, in spite of her upbringing, she became a lovely, gracious, caring woman who never forgot what it felt like to be poor and needy. I treasure her memory and the example she set.

Barbie's Elopement or The Pink Pig Says I Do

by Sandra Chastain

If you love them, let them go. If they return, they were always yours. If they don't, they never were.
—*Anonymous*

I never see a pig that I don't think of weddings and the summer of 1948.

Southern weddings have always been *events*, though not the kind we see on television where there are expensive invitations, exotic floral decorations, lavish dinners, and receptions. When I was growing up, the florist decorated with waxy green smilax vines pulled from the woods, candles, and whichever flower was in season.

The true measure of your social position was the number of attendants in the wedding. The more bridesmaids, the more popular the bride. The end result was most girls filled a closet in their house with once-used bridesmaid gowns. The bride's selection of the dress was invariably accompanied with the familiar phrase, "It's a little expensive, but it can *definitely* be worn again." It was, and it couldn't.

All of this preparation led to a picture of the bride and groom coming down the aisle after the ceremony and a half page retelling of the event and the showers that led up to it in the Wadley Herald. Every bride knew there were more subscribers to the weekly paper than people who lived in town. It could even be considered the first chain letter.

To me, weddings were the ultimate fantasy. In grammar school, while my friends were in the woods playing Tarzan and Jane, we performed plays on Connie Hayes's stage-high front porch. I used a piece of net left over from making a crinoline petticoat and satin drapery material to become a bride.

From childhood dress-up, the girls moved on to Home Economics and Future Homemakers of America and the ultimate hero-crush on an older girl you wanted to emulate. Trust me, these girls were the first real Barbies. We put them on a pedestal and waited for the secrets of boys, romance, and womanhood to be revealed. My Barbie was eighteen and lived across the street. Long legged, black-eyed, she had dark shiny hair she rolled in pin curls at night and tied back by a ribbon or fastened with a barrette.

Her name was Rose Robertson, but she insisted with dramatic flair that everyone call her 'Irish.' That's another thing, as a measure of your popularity, nicknames were almost as important as the number of attendants you had in the wedding. Irish made up her own nickname in fourth grade. That's when she first saw Dink Langlin. She's been planning her wedding ever since.

As captain of the Wadley Dragons cheerleading squad, Miss Wadley High School, and the president of the Future Homemakers, she was willing to wait. Each event brought her a step closer to Dink and marriage.

The Germans were marching across Europe by the time they graduated. But that didn't touch us until the Japanese attacked Pearl Harbor. Dink, along with most of the young men in town, signed up to save the world. Once he enlisted, Irish was caught up in the excitement. When he was settled in a far-away Army post, they'd marry, and she'd follow him. But it didn't work that way. The only 'Irish' Dink took with him was a curled black and white snapshot of a dreamy-eyed girl leaning against the side of a car, her foot on the running board and her skirt pulled up to expose her long legs. A scarf was tied around her neck calling attention to her chest pushed out ever so slightly against the thin sweater she was wearing. Betty Grable had nothing on Irish Robertson.

I was twelve when Irish grew tired of waiting for Dink and even more tired of missing out on what was going on in the world. She broke my heart by running away to Atlanta, explaining that she was only doing her patriotic duty by taking a job in the bomber plant. No more watching her studying the movie magazines for new hairstyles or helping her dress and apply her make-up for a date who was only standing in for Dink. She rarely visited home, since gas was rationed, and men and women in the service were given first choice of seats on the bus. Then the war ended, and our "boys" returned and took back their jobs. Irish stayed on in Atlanta for a year before she came finally came home. By that time I was sixteen and reading *Seventeen* magazine while I dreamed of marrying Jeff Coleman who delivered Merita bread to Archie's Grocery, where I worked part time. The day Irish came home she took me up to her room and showed me her engagement ring.

"Oh, Irish, did Dink finally propose?"

"Dink? Of course not. He's a child. You don't know this man."

"Who is he?" I asked breathlessly as I collapsed on the floor at her feet.

"I shouldn't tell you," she said, dancing around the room to the humming of the wedding march. "I haven't told my mama and daddy yet."

"Tell me! Tell me," I pleaded.

"All right. I've met a *real* man, a sophisticated banker from Mobile. His family is one of the first families of Alabama. They belong to a country club and play golf and . . . he's tall and he wants to marry me."

"When are you getting married?"

"As soon as we can arrange the wedding. I have to get a dress and choose my bridesmaids and pick out china and crystal. But first, I have to tell Mama."

"What about your daddy? Mr. McKay won't like him being from Alabama."

"Yes, I have to tell him, too." She sank down on the bed, the smile on her face turning into an expression of worry. "And he's going to say no. I'm sure of it. Oh, Joanna, what am I going to do? I don't want to live here and join the Missionary Society and work in the bank. I desperately want to marry James. Suppose daddy won't agree?"

"You could elope," I suggested. "You're over twenty-one."

"I would, but James won't hear of it. His family expects a church wedding. I just have to convince Mama and Daddy. I'll do it tonight, but you have to stay for supper. I need moral support."

"But won't they think that's strange, me being here when you're telling them something so personal?"

"You're always here, Joanna. Mama looks at you as a second daughter. They won't even notice. Please?"

I wasn't comfortable with her request, but I could never refuse Irish. I'd been her shadow for too many years. Besides, this was the juiciest event since Louisa Bedingfield eloped with the mailman the night of her high school graduation.

Irish waited until her mother served her lemon ice box pie and started to clear the table. "Mama, wait a minute please. I have to tell you and Daddy something." She started off slow, "I'm engaged," then finished in a rush with, "And I'm getting married."

There was complete silence.

Her mother sank down in her chair, still holding the stack of desert plates. She asked, "Who are you marrying?"

"You don't know him, he's from Alabama," Irish answered.

Miss Willa set the plates on the table. "Why isn't he here with you?" she asked.

"He's gone home to tell his parents while I tell you. I thought we could start making plans. You'll meet him when he comes for me in two weeks. Then I'll go over for a visit with my future in-laws."

Mr. McKay pushed his chair back from the table. "There will be no wedding plans until the boy talks to me," he growled.

"He's not a boy," Irish protested. "He's a man, the kind of man I want to marry. Don't embarrass me, Daddy. He comes from an old family in Mobile, Alabama."

"So?" Miss Willa snapped, something she rarely did. "I come from an old family here in Wadley, Georgia. What makes him so special?"

"Well he's very handsome. He's well-to-do. He's going to buy me a house, and . . . he . . . Mama, he wears suits and . . . gets manicures."

I saw her daddy wince when she mentioned manicures. You see, he lost two fingers in an accident in the box factory. After they ran out of wood and cardboard during the depression, Mr. McKay opened a service station where he sold more service than gas—gas being in short supply. Most of the folks in town would have been reduced to walking if not for Mr. McKay's skill at improvising car parts. He made a living, but the grease under his fingernails became his permanent medal of honor. We didn't have a manicurist, and no man in Wadley would ever have been seen getting a manicure anyway.

That's when everything went crazy. Mr. McKay stood and left the table and Miss Willa followed him. With great sympathy, I comforted Irish afterward. She spent the next hour crying, bathing her swollen eyes, while I pumped her for all the delicious details of their courtship. Then she sent me home, closed her bedroom door and refused to come out until her daddy agreed to be nice to her fiancé.

The next day Irish was still locked in her room. Miss Willa and her neighbors from either side, Nettie Mills and Thelma Chandler sat on the veranda snapping green beans and talked about what ought to be done. I discovered that if I sat in the back and kept quiet, the women forgot I was there.

"Willa, I don't know why McKay is so against Rose marrying," Miss Nettie said. "He's just gonna make them run away like you and McKay did."

Miss Willa and McKay eloped? That was grown-up news to me.

"We didn't run away," Miss Willa said. "Everybody went off and got married during the depression."

"You didn't *just* go off and get married; your elopement was a pure work of art," Nettie argued. "I was there, remember? I'm the one who came to spend the night with you—supposedly to help you in your mama's and daddy's café. I'm the one who packed your clothes in with mine so you could smuggle them out of the house."

Thelma Chandler dropped all pretense of snapping beans. She was the only outsider in the group, having lived in Louisville, the next town, before she married a local farmer. "Tell me about your wedding."

"I might as well," Miss Willa said, "before it was over, everybody in town was involved in the elopement. It all happened because my mother didn't want me to get married. Back then, my folks didn't really have a café, they sold barbecue, gas when people had money to buy it and cigarettes. Mama needed my help to pump the gas. She didn't like the smell of it on her hands."

"She needed your help," Nettie agreed, "but that wasn't the only reason. She just plain didn't like McKay. Never understood that. He might have been a little wild but he had a job when a lot of men didn't until the box factory closed. Kept him and you out of the soup lines."

"We didn't have any soup lines," Willa said. In Wadley, people look after each other."

"That's just another way of saying they get into everybody else's business," Thelma said. "Get back to the elopement. How'd you manage to get away that day?"

"It was almost dark. Roger Alston and Pete Hawkins drove out to the café on the highway south of town and pulled up to the door. They blew the horn for gas and I ran out to pump fifty cents worth. Pete wanted a pack of Lucky Strike cigarettes and gave me the money. I put the money in the drawer and took out his change. "The man wants cigarettes, Mama," I said, and waited until my mother looked away. Then I ran back to the car. When I got there, Roger opened the back door and pulled me in."

I was never sure he had to do it, but he pulled off like the sheriff was after us. Before we got out of sight, Mama and Daddy had closed the restaurant door and pulled in right behind us. They would have caught us but daddy's Model T gave out of gas just as it reached the bridge over Boggy Gut Creek. Like I said, Mama didn't like the smell of gas on her hands so making sure the tank was full was my responsibility. I must have forgotten to do it."

Thelma nodded. "Smart girl. That's what I would have done, too. Go on."

Miss Willa continued, "The plan was to meet up with McKay at Nettie's house. But Mama and Daddy managed to get a ride with Mr. Raines and when we saw him gaining on us in his beat up old truck, we knew we were in trouble. Everybody in the county knew that the truck could fly. That's how he escaped the law when he made his weekly run over to Augusta delivering moonshine."

"Did he catch you?" Thelma asked.

"No, about that time we came up on the cemetery on the right, dark and spooky in the moonlight. Roger pulled in. 'Get out, Willa. Hide behind Rachel Steven's angel tombstone and we'll come back for you,' he said.

"I had what my Mother called a "Come to Jesus" moment. Cemeteries scared me to death in the daytime. At night they were Halloween's worst ghost story come to life. The cemetery was full of crickets chirping, frogs croaking and the movement of small animals. Was being Mrs. McKay Robertson worth it? I almost changed my mind."

"But she didn't," Nettie took up the story. "Lois Battle came and got me at the café, and we headed to my house. McKay was there, but Willa wasn't. He was sure that your folks had caught you, Willa. It was all we could do to keep him from going after you."

"About that time I was wishing you had. Mr. Raines's truck stopped in front of the cemetery, and I could hear my daddy cussing. Mama wanted Mr. Raines to take them to the sheriff's office, but he wouldn't, even when daddy offered to pay him. Said if the law looked in his truck, his fine would cost more than daddy's bribe. Daddy stomped around in the dark at one point, heading straight for me."

I'd been quiet until then, as mesmerized as Thelma. "What stopped him?" I blurted out before I thought. But Miss Willa was into the telling now, and I could see that this was her moment of glory. She didn't even look at me.

"An owl lit on Rachel Steven's angel's left arm and hooted every time I moved. Daddy seemed to focus on the bird for a moment then climbed back in the truck. McKay never knew it, but when we stopped for me to change into the suit I was married in it was for a totally different reason that I'd planned."

"So, you managed to get away," Thelma said.

"Yes. Once they came back for me, we formed a caravan, the boys in Roger's car and the girls in Lois's and headed for the Justice of the Peace. After the wedding, Roger and Pete got in the car with Lois and went home. McKay and I went on to Augusta."

"And what happened?" Nettie asked. "You never did tell us."

"And I never will," Willa said sharply. "Let's get these beans snapped." She sighed. "I may not agree, but I've guess we got to start making plans for this wedding."

"You think McKay will go along with Irish marrying this man?" Thelma asked.

"McKay's a stubborn fool. He wanted Irish to marry Dink, but if she's found somebody else...If it takes a trip to Augusta to force him to be civil to Irish's intended, we'll go."

Nettie frowned. "What's in Augusta that will change his mind?"

Willa smiled. "The Blue Bird Motel."

I don't know who let the secret out. It certainly wasn't me. I'd sworn to Irish on my honor to keep it quiet. If the town found out that Irish came home to get married to a stranger,

I certainly didn't tell them. But I owed it to Irish to let them know what a fine catch he was.

When Jeff Coleman stopped by the store on Saturday night to take me to a movie, I knew it was safe to tell him. Louisville, where he lived, was ten miles away.

"Sounds like she's moving up in the world," he said. "I'd marry a woman with money over somebody in Jefferson County anytime."

Well, that let me out. I'd never have money. But I had another reason for questioning Irish's choice. "I wonder if she really loves him? She always said she'd marry Dink."

"And who's Dink?"

"He's a great looking guy she went to school with. Everybody knew they'd get married. But he joined the Army and said they had to wait until he was assigned to a post. Then he became a pilot and went to Europe."

"So, what happened?"

"Irish said if he didn't marry her before he left, she wouldn't wait. I don't know what happened, but I think they were both sorry they broke up. Irish waited for a while, but when he didn't send for her, she returned his class ring. Then he got shot down, and he's been in the hospital for a long time."

We were sitting in Jeff's truck at the only traffic light in town when the Greyhound Bus pulled in and several passengers got off. One of them was wearing a uniform. As we watched, he dug his duffle bag out of the luggage compartment and threw it over his shoulder. When he crossed the street and the railroad tracks, I realized who it was. "Oh, my goodness, Jeff, that's him; that's Dink Langlin. Quick, take me home. I have to tell Irish."

"But we're going to the drive-in movie and . . ."

Make out. I knew what he was thinking and I was having a hard time heading him off. I was having a harder time saying no. It wasn't that I wasn't interested. I was more than interested. But being with Irish had made me catch a little of her excitement about getting out of a little town that was slowly drying up.

"Quick, let's give Dink a ride. He ought to know that Irish is here and . . . engaged. I mean somebody ought to tell him, don't you think?"

I can't say that Jeff was in agreement, but he quickly saw that his plans were being put on hold. The sooner I was satisfied, the sooner he would be. He turned the truck around and drove back toward Dink.

"Does he know you?" he asked. "He certainly won't know me."

"Sure," I said, hoping that at least he'd know my name when I quickly called out, "Hi, Dink. You remember me, Joanna Scott, Irish's friend."

He stopped and looked into the truck. "You're little Joanna?"

"Well, I'm not so little anymore. Get in. We'll give you a ride."

Dink threw his bag into the back and climbed in.

"This is my boyfriend, Jeff," I said. "Your mama said you've been . . .sick. I know they'll be glad you're home. I . . . I think you ought to know. . ." I babbled on, "I mean you might want to know that Irish is kinda home on leave, too."

He didn't say anything. Maybe this was a bad idea. No, he needed to know. Irish would want him to know. "And she's getting married," I added in a rush. "Not that Mr. McKay has agreed. Miss Willa said he wanted Irish to marry you."

Dink reached inside his shirt pocket and pulled out a pack of cigarettes. "Oh? Who's she going to marry?" he asked a little too casual for the shake of the lighter he was holding.

"Some man from Alabama, a banker, I think, but Mr. McKay won't give her permission until he talks to the man.

I can't imagine what Mr. McKay's gonna say."

"I can," Dink said with a dry laugh. "The same thing he said to me when I asked for Irish's hand. 'What you gonna give me in exchange?'"

Jeff drove slowly up Main Street and turned right on the Midville Road. "You're kidding," he said as he turned into the sandy yard next to the Langlin house.

"Nope. As I recall, we settled on a pig."

The porch light came on, and Mr. and Mrs. Langlin came outside. When they realized who it was, Mr. John came down the steps and shook Dink's hand, pulling him into a quick hug. Miss Bertha was crying and laughing and wiping her hands on her apron. "Oh, my goodness, son," she said. "You could have let me know. I'd have fried some chicken. All I'd planned on for supper was cornbread and soup beans."

They were still hugging when Jeff backed out. "You know we're going to be late for the movie," he said. "If I get a ticket, you're going to pay it."

"You're not going to get a ticket because we aren't going. Drive back to Irish's house. I have to tell her that Dink's home."

"I don't think this is a good idea. Besides, what about us? We won't see each other again until next weekend." He put his arm around my shoulder and pulled me close.

"Stop that, Jeff. Somebody will tell my mama."

"That's what you always say," he said in a tight voice. "I don't know why you're getting so heated up about Irish's wedding. Don't I turn you on?"

"When we get married is time enough for me to get turned on."

"Then let's get married," he said. "We can be in South Carolina by morning. Don't have to have no special papers to get married there."

"Run off?"

"Elope. That's all you been talking about. First Mr. McKay and Miss Willa. Now, Dink is back, and I can just see your mind working. You're ready to help them elope right now. Aren't you?"

When I didn't answer he popped the clutch and gave the truck gas. There was a screeching sound that would certainly get back to my mama as he drove off down the highway. I didn't want to admit that I'd been getting turned on for a while. But Mama didn't like Jeff. Said he wasn't ambitious enough. I couldn't count on him. And of late, I kept thinking about Irish going to Atlanta and finding a job where she could earn money and live in a home for girls where she had a roommate and someone to go to the movies with. I couldn't stop imagining myself there.

Jeff stopped in front of my house. He didn't get out of the truck and open my door. He didn't try to kiss me again or touch my breasts. He just waited. I got out by myself and watched him roar off. I was already beginning to wonder if I'd done the right thing by turning him down tonight. There weren't many boys in Wadley. I was lucky to have Jeff.

Or, maybe I didn't have him any more.

Irish was in her room planning what she was going to wear when James came. "If I dress up like I would have in Atlanta, I'll make Mama and Daddy uncomfortable. They'll look bad." She sighed. "Chances are that James will make them uncomfortable anyway."

"Why would he?" I asked. I couldn't imagine Irish picking out any man who'd make her parents look bad.

"I mean, he'll wear a suit and he'll probably bring Mama flowers."

"Well, just tell him not to do that," I suggested, thinking how heavenly it would be to have a man bring flowers.

"I did. He wouldn't hear of it. He wants to make a good impression. It was either make him feel good or make them feel bad. Oh, Joanna, what am I going to do? You're right; I'll feel uncomfortable meeting his parents, too. We ought to just elope."

"Irish, I have something to tell you that you ought to know."

She must have caught the reluctance in my voice. "What? Tell me now or I'll stick pins in your voodoo doll."

My voodoo doll? Buying the dolls from a gypsy at the county fair had been a joke. Of course we never really believed in Ouija boards or voodoo or any of that stuff. Still, a ripple ran down my spine.

"Joanne?"

"It's Dink," I said. "He's home."

"How do you know?"

"Jeff and I . . . we were going to the drive-in, and we saw him get off the bus. We drove him to his mama's house. He must be over his injury; he sure does look good in a uniform. I don't know how you let him get away."

"Because . . . he left me here and didn't care how lonesome I was. I could have gone with him to the Army base, made friends with the other wives. . .seen the world. But no. I had to wait for him until he'd stopped the Germans."

"But you did see some of the world, didn't you? You went to Atlanta and had an exciting life. I'll bet you spent every night at the USO club."

"Well, I did do my part to entertain our boys. I thought it was my duty. Do you think Dink cared? No."

"How do you know what he thought?"

"Because I wrote to him and told him everything I was doing."

"And he didn't answer you back?"

"Yes. He told me to have fun. He said I was young and deserved to spread my wings. When he got assigned to the Air Corps he didn't even ask me to come to see him get his wings. I didn't have an engagement ring, Joanne, but I so wanted him to pin me with his wings."

"Well, you've got James," I offered.

"James, oh my gosh, what am I going to do? I have to see Dink. Why don't his mother and daddy have a telephone?" She was still walking around the room but her gait had changed from bridal pace to military march. "Did he say how long he was going to stay?"

"No, but I think he's going to talk to your daddy. I mean, I just got that idea."

Irish went to her closet and started studying her clothes. I couldn't decide whether she was getting ready for James or Dink but when she pulled out a sundress with a stretchy top, I had a bad feeling about what was coming.

When I left, she was sitting on the veranda in the dark, waiting. I watched until I couldn't keep my eyes open but I never saw anybody come. Finally the house lights went out.

The next day was Sunday. I was still asleep when I heard the scream. In fact half of Wadley heard the scream. By the time I pulled on my jeans and hit the street a crowd of neighbors had gathered around the front steps of Irish's house.

"How could he? How could he?" Irish was clasping and unclasping her fists giving her best Betty Davis impression of a woman on the edge.

I pushed my way through the onlookers to see what they were laughing about. Right there on the sidewalk, in front of God and all the neighbors, was a wooden crate containing a large pink pig. Judging by the oinking, the pig seemed to be enjoying the hoo-rah.

"Hush up, girl," Mr. McKay said to Irish as he opened the screen and stepped out.

"But, Daddy . . ."

"Either hush, or go back inside." He knelt down beside the crate and grinned.

"Guess the pig's a girl," the eight year old who lived next door said.

"This one is, but lots of pigs start out pink," Mr. McKay said. "They grow up and turn white or their spots come out.

"She has a pink bow around her neck," one of the bystanders said.

"There's a note attached. It's addressed to Mr. McKay," Bob Crane observed. "What's it say, McKay?"

"I think it's an offer for my daughter's hand in marriage," Mr. McKay said and reached inside for the note.

"Oh!" Irish exploded, before turning to run back into the house. "Mother!"

By church time the story was all over town. Irish's new fiancé had sent a gift, earnest money, Mr. Crane said. Like the Indians used to do when they had to pay for a bride with horses or skins. Knowing Mr. McKay, everybody seemed to think it was a clever thing for an outsider to do. I didn't say anything but I was pretty sure I knew who'd sent the pig, and Irish knew, too. I wondered how he managed to get up so early and pull this off without a car. It was years later that I found out Jeff had helped Dink.

The pig went to Mr. McKay's brother Sloan's farm and Irish went to her room. Dink never approached Irish and Irish swore if he did, she'd tell him in no uncertain terms to "Go to grass and eat mullet." Nobody knew what that actually meant, short of an unpleasant trip from which a person didn't return.

By Wednesday, I was beginning to worry. James was coming for the weekend. Dink only had three days more of leave before he had to report to an airbase in Texas. The first really hot spell of the summer came, and the town seemed to hold its breath. The two-block-long business section of Wadley had more weekday business than it ever experienced. The bank normally closed on Wednesday afternoon because it opened on Saturday morning. This week it stayed open. The news that a stranger had checked into the Wadley Hotel ran up the street like lightening following an electric wire into the house. My friend Rachel and I walked downtown and staked a table at the drugstore. We ordered cherry cola's and made them last an hour as we waited.

"That must be her fiancé James," I said. "What are we going to do, Rachel? She doesn't love him. She just wants to marry a rich important man. It's Dink she loves. Always has."

"I wouldn't love him if he went off and left me."

"My mama said he thought he'd die and he didn't want to leave her a widow." My mama always took up for Dink.

"That's silly," Rachel said, laying the back of her hand dramatically against her forehead. Her Betty Davis routine didn't hold a candle to Irish's.

I sprang to my feet. "Let's go, Rachel."

"Where?"

"To see Dink. He needs to know about James."

We raced up the street to the intersection and turned right. The Langlins were sitting on the side porch. I could hear them laughing. Dink's sister Lurlene's car was in the yard.

"Uh oh, Rachel, they've got company. How are we going to get Dink away?"

"I don't know," she said. "This was your idea."

"I know, as you start up the steps, you fall. You'll sprain your ankle and we'll get Dink to take us home."

"I can't do that," Rachel argued. "I'm no good at physical things."

Then I heard someone heading around the wrap-around porch toward us. It was Dink. Now or never. I danced up the steps, caught my toe on the edge and fell backward, letting out a yell as I hit the ground.

"Joanne." Dink ran toward me. "Are you hurt?"

I groaned and fell back. "I think I've sprained my ankle."

"Let me get some help," he said.

"Could you just take me home?"

By that time the others were gathered around me. "Of course," Miss Lurlene said and pulled her car keys from her pocket. "You drive, Dink. I'll come with you."

"No!" I protested and attempted to stand. This time my groan was no dramatic gesture. I leaned toward Dink, motioning for him to bend down. "Get me out quick. I have something private to tell you that's a matter of life and death. Open the door, Rachel."

He looked puzzled for a moment then lifted me and slid me onto the front seat. I bit back a cry of pain. "Hurry," I said and pulled the door closed.

Less than five minutes later we were at my house, across the street from Irish's. "Dink, Irish's fiancé just checked into the hotel. If you're going to marry Irish, you'd better go get her right now. You can drive over to Augusta and elope, just like Mr. McKay and Miss Willa."

He looked down at me for a minute and grinned. "They did, huh? That old liar. He made me promise not to marry Irish until I got back."

"He did? Well, you're back. I don't think I'd wait any longer." I said and opened my door to encourage him to take quick action. This time I touched my foot to the pavement and crumpled to the ground.

"You can stop acting now, Joanne," Rachel said.

"I'm not acting," I moaned and whispered under my breath, "Just help me up, Rachel and I'll jump to the steps on my good ankle. Then go call Daddy, and tell him to come home." I raised my voice and said, "Hurry, Dink, before *someone* comes."

I swallowed the pain long enough to see Dink march into Irish's house. I could hear him talking as he headed up the steps. Then there was silence. Moments later, Dink, carrying Irish who was holding a small suitcase, came out and got into the car.

Miss Willa followed them, beaming like Brother Colson when someone came down to the altar to confess a sin. I could hear her call after them as they drove away, "I recommend the Blue Bird Motel."

Irish never knew that the man who checked into the Wadley Hotel was a shoe salesman from Des Moines. Miss Lurlene always claimed credit for the church wedding that followed Irish's marriage by the justice of the peace. A second ceremony was the price of lending Dink her car. The bridal procession took a little longer than usual because Irish insisted that as her maid of honor, I be allowed to walk down the aisle on crutches. Mr. McKay even announced that he was paying the doctor for setting my broken ankle. It was worth it. And I didn't even have to wear an expensive gown.

Mr. and Mrs. Dink Langlin had a full page spread in the Wadley Herald, describing the two weddings and their relocation to Texas. The editor's column carried the story of the pig right next to an ad for Clete's new barbecue stand. The following week a note from the publisher explained that the placement was just unfortunate. Clete raised his own hogs.

I gave some serious thought to elopement but in the end both Rachel and I went to Augusta and enrolled in business school. Jeff took a course in television repair and we are having a church wedding.

He's already made a reservation at the Blue Bird Motel.

By the way, Sweet Pea, that's what Mr. McKay named his sow, weighs 300 pounds now and has set a tradition; every prospective father-in-law in Wadley asks for a pink pig in exchange for the bride. I told Jeff he'd better not bring my daddy any pig. He just smiled. My daddy doesn't hunt but he and Jeff are building a dog yard in the back corner of Daddy's property, complete with a very large water trough.

Well, this is the South and it's hot down here.

Drag Racer Arrested On Horseback

by Virginia Ellis

"O, for a horse with wings!"
—Cymbeline Act 2

My boyfriend during high school was a drag racer. You know how we in the South love our cars. (Think of the General Lee on *The Dukes of Hazard.*) Anyway, I could sort of understand his need for speed, since I was into racing of a different sort. Instead of many-horse power, I depended on one quarter-horse barrel racer to ride to fame and fortune—or at least a colorful blue ribbon and trophy with a miniature horse on the top.

Usually our two racing hobbies didn't cross paths, so to say. Drag races were mostly held on Saturday nights "under the lights" while the big day for rodeo-ing is Sunday. My boyfriend rarely went by horseback, whereas Saturday night being "date night" I spent a good deal of time scrunched up against the gear shift in his '57 Ford or later, his '62 Corvette.

There was one Sunday though, where our two worlds collided, figuratively speaking, thank goodness. The occasion happened at an amateur drag racing event. By amateur, I mean unsanctioned by the law. In all other respects these good old boys were dead serious about their racing—there was real money wagered on the outcome. So, hearing about the gathering through word of mouth—no internet blogs in those days—my boyfriend decided to show up and try his luck. Since I usually spent Sunday riding, I decided to meet him there, to ride my horse over to the abandoned airstrip serving as racetrack and watch.

That was my first mistake. Let me backtrack a bit and tell you a little more about my horse. In order to be a good barrel racer, a horse has to have short bursts of speed coupled with the ability to nearly sit down and turn on a dime. It has to have good eyesight and be able to pay attention to pressure on a rein, a knee, or feel the rider lean one way or the other. My horse had all that. But, as with all creatures being a mix of good and bad, he had a few other things, too.

He hated being inside the rodeo arena. He'd plod around, sneak mouthfuls of grass and basically "hang loose," perfectly happy *outside* the high plank gate to the inner arena. But as soon as that gate opened and I nudged him toward it—all bets were off.

The secret was not to stop.

Have you seen barrel races on TV where the women have their horses at a full gallop before the cameras even see them? They fly out of the bowels of the arena like runaway trains. Now they *might* be working on a better time, but they also might be depriving their horses of too many decisions. Decisions like, *Do I really want to do this*?

There's a term for it—ring sour. My horse, if given a choice, would turn around and climb over the fence rather than go into the ring for the 25 or so seconds it took to run the barrel course. Maybe he didn't like the people watching, or the way the announcers pronounced his name. I'll never know.

Anyway, he could assert his independence of my meager control at any time. He never dumped me in the dirt in front of all those spectators, but we came close a couple of times. The worst was when we flew through the gate, aimed across the arena toward the first barrel when the no-time buzzer sounded. I pulled up as the announcer informed the crowd—and me—that the timers were down. They'd have them fixed as soon as possible.

Well, that left me, and my adrenalin-pumping horse in the middle of a place he absolutely *did not* want to be. Once my horse was primed to run, waiting left his mindset. I can't imagine the look on my face. There was no talking him down. First he backed toward the gate, then, in a term called *crow-hopping,* he sidestepped his way toward the gate. I could practically hear his mind working, *If I can just get to the gate, I can get rid of her and climb out.*

My only option was to spin him in circles. So we did that, him spinning, me praying and spinning, while two cowboys scratched their heads on how come the timers weren't doing what they were supposed to do. We were within ten feet of the dreaded gate when the buzzer went off again and the announcer said the timers were fixed. Needless to say after all that nervous spinning, we didn't even place that day. I was just glad to live through it.

I don't want you to think my horse wasn't very smart, because in many ways, he was. He proved it when he decided to be an escape artist. If a fence stood between him and another horse he liked, or greener grass, he would press his chest against it to measure the height—then, if it was doable, he would casually leap over it. He also knew his way around our small town. When I moved him from one ranch to another approximately eight miles away, he just jumped the fence and made his way back to his original home. In order to do that, he had to cross two roads with moderate traffic and a bridge over a river. I used to wonder if he even stopped at the red lights and looked both ways.

Now I've made him sound crazy when in many ways he was a gentleman. He never bit, kicked or bucked. He'd take the bit easy. He didn't crib or break reins. Once when he reared up and I fell underneath him, he stood absolutely still, even turning to look under his belly like, *What the heck are you doin' down there?*

But he hated thunder, or any loud noise, for that matter. A crack of booming Florida thunder had put me off his back and onto my own butt a few times. It's amazing how a two thousand pound animal can bunch up and disappear out from under you in a split second—an example of that speed I was talking about before. The problem with horses, however, is that they often jump in the absolute wrong direction. A big yellow school bus with screeching brakes should be something any horse should want to avoid—instead he did his best, over my objections, to run in front of it in a panic.

Now that would bring me back to our adventure in attending the drag races. Silly me, it never occurred to me that my horse had never been to a real tire-squealing, smoke-belching, jet-engine-sounding drag race. Thinking back, maybe it was my own IQ that needed testing.

Well, my horse and I showed up just in time for the first race. I joined the group of spectators, guys who'd come along to bet or watch mixed with a few other racers' girlfriends, standing off to the side. Needless to say, I was the only person on horseback. The racers themselves were gathered around the cars of the competition—looking at engines, talking horsepower. My boyfriend waved once from his car but didn't come over right away. With a help of a friend of his, he was removing the baffles on the headers of his '57 Ford—sort of like taking the muffler off a car. It made the car go faster—something to do with airflow—and it also made the engine sound like a roaring beast on steroids.

My horse did fairly well as the first two racers squealed off the starting line. His ears twitched back and forth, and he seemed to stiffen up—ready to jump. I talked to him, rubbed between his ears trying to distract him. I don't know how much he heard me over the engines. The next two cars had him stepping sideways—and you guessed it—moving directly for the starting line. I was beginning to realize that hanging around drag racing was a bad idea. Finally, in the hopes of calming him down I dismounted, determined to keep him from pulling away from me. It was a last resort. Contrary to popular belief, most times—unless you're The Horse Whisperer—it's easier to control a horse when you're on his back than when you're standing next to him.

Well, it was my boyfriend's turn to race then and, glory be, my horse kept his ears flat back and his butt bunched up, but he didn't make a break for it. Maybe he decided since my boots were on the ground he wouldn't be required to do any racing himself. And he was okay with that.

Of course my boyfriend won his race. He pulled his car off the pavement on the back side of the starting line, collected his winnings, and came over to see me.

That's when we heard the sirens.

Police cars arriving in the middle of an illegal drag race is like rocks thrown at a hornet's nest. People ran in every direction, cars spun in the dirt and smoked tires on the asphalt. I had all I could do to hold on to my horse, so I decided to remount with the help of my boyfriend. Since he was too far away from his car to make a run for it, he climbed up behind me. We were doing our best to look like innocent bystanders while the police looked over the cars they'd caught and pulled drivers out for a trip to jail.

We should've used my one horsepower to make like a tree and leave, but alas, my boyfriend didn't want to abandon his car to the tow trucks if he didn't have to. So we hung around watching the commotion. Unfortunately, it gave one policeman time to notice us, and he waved us over.

"What are you two doing out here?" He gave my horse a wide berth.

"Watching the races," my boyfriend answered.

"You have any idea who owns that yellow and white '57 Ford over there?"

"No, sir," my boyfriend said.

The policeman looked at me and I shook my head. I was hoping it wasn't really a lie if I didn't say anything out loud.

Then he asked for my boyfriend's driver's license.

Well, it didn't take long to run the car plates and match them up to my boyfriend. When the policeman walked back over he said he'd have to take him in for racing.

"I was only watching."

"Then why are the headers opened up? You can't drive it that way on the street."

It was kind of hard to explain to my boyfriend's parents how he happened to get arrested off the back of my horse, but there you have it—life in a small town. At least he'd made enough money by winning his race to pay the fine.

As for my horse, that was the last time I ever took him to a drag race. I could tell he hadn't enjoyed it much even though we'd become part of local legend. *Drag Racer Arrested On Horseback.*

It had been a nerve-wracking day for all concerned. My horse and I did have quite an adventure at a local Halloween carnival the next year, but that's a story for another day. Just take my advice—never try to put a sheet on a horse.

DINNER ON THE GROUNDS

The authors of *More Sweet Tea* hope you will enjoy the following tastes of down-home cooking from family kitchens across the South.

Table of Contents:

Fly By Night

Sarah Addison Allen

Great Aunt Sophie's Pennies From Heaven

Ingredients:

2 sticks of margarine
1/2 lb. sharp cheddar cheese (grated)
2 cups plain flour
1/4 teaspoon cayenne pepper
1 teaspoon salt
3 cups Rice Krispies

Directions:

Cream the cheese and margarine together. Sift the dry ingredients, then add to the cheese mixture. Stir in the Rice Krispies and mix well. Roll into 1" balls and put on a baking sheet, then flatten each ball with the back of a spoon. Bake at 400 degrees for 8 minutes. They will be crisp and cookie-like, but with a bite.

Hair Today, Gone Tomorrow

Maureen Hardegree

Lucille's Fried Pies

(Makes 8)

INGREDIENTS:

1 package of dried apples or peaches (You can use fresh apples or peaches, but you gotta cook 'em down.)
2 cups of water
1/4 cup of granulated sugar (to sweeten)
1/4 cup of dark brown sugar (to sweeten and flavor)
5 pinches of cinnamon (also for flavor, but you know in the old days, folks didn't have the money to buy spices like cinnamon)
1 teaspoon of cornstarch (to make the liquid in the filling thicken)
1 can of flaky, layered biscuits (If I don't make my own dough anymore, why in the H-E-double-L should you?)
Powdered Sugar

DIRECTIONS:

The night before, you've got to cook your dried apples down. For those of you who don't know, cooking down means you put those apples in a pot with some water and cook them until most of that water's gone. When they look almost like fresh apples, you can add your sugar and spice and cornstarch. Once the apples cool, mash them up. I use a potato masher. You can use whatever fancy utensil you got. Cover them and put them in the refrigerator overnight. (The filling isn't as messy when it's cold.)

The next day, you've got to figure how you want to cook these pies. The old folks cooked them in lard (or shortening) in a well-seasoned cast-iron skillet on top of the stove. You can only fry two at a time that way. If you use the cast iron skillet, set the lard to melting, keep it on medium high when you're ready to fry the pies, and turn them over to get the top brown once the underside is done—about 7-10 minutes depending on your stove. An easier way is to oven-fry those pies. All you do is pour a little vegetable oil in the bottom of a cookie sheet (Don't use olive oil. It won't taste right.) and set your oven to 350 degrees.

While your oven's warming, roll out your biscuits on a floured surface until they're as big as a saucer. Wet the outer edges of that circle so the pie won't open up while they're cooking. Spoon two heaping tablespoons of that cold fruit filling in the center, then fold one side over the other, covering the filling and making a half-moon. Mash down where the edges meet with the tines of a fork. Spread some butter or oil on the tops of the pies, prick the tops of the pies with that same fork, then either fry them in the cast iron skillet or stick them in the long pan/cookie sheet and bake them until the bottoms are good and brown, about 7-10 minutes. Flip the pies over and fry for another 5-7 minutes, until both sides are brown. Remove from pan onto some paper towels to absorb the excess oil and set them to cool.

Once they're cool, dust them with a pinch or so of powdered sugar. I'm not one to put on the dog, but they look right pretty with a little sugar on top.

The Fan Dancer

Bert Goolsby

Raw Apple and Pear Cake

INGREDIENTS:
2 and 1/2 cups flour
4 eggs
2 cups sugar
1 and 1/2 cups cooking oil
1 teaspoon cinnamon
1 teaspoon vanilla
2 teaspoons baking powder
1 cup chopped pecans
1 teaspoon salt
3 cups chopped raw apples and pears

GLAZE:
1 tablespoon milk
1/2 cup of powdered sugar

DIRECTIONS:

Mix all dry ingredients. Add eggs. Slowly pour in cooking oil, beating constantly. Add vanilla. Fold in apples and pecans. Bake in oven in a greased tube pan for one hour at 350 degrees. Mix milk and sugar together and drizzle over the cake while the cake is warm. For an added treat, serve warm and topped with whipped cream.

The Healing Touch

Susan Alvis

Citrus Cooler Cookies

(Aunt Agnes developed these little cookies after she gave up concocting medicines. She says they are just the right cooling taste for the hottest of afternoons. Serve with a glass of iced tea.)

Ingredients:
1and 1/2 cups of room temperature, softened butter
1/2 cup of sugar
1/2 teaspoon of vanilla extract
1/2 teaspoon of lemon extract (or orange)
1 teaspoon of grated orange peel
3 cups of all purpose flour
1and 1/4 cups of chopped nuts (walnuts or pecans)

Directions:

Cream together butter, flavorings and sugar. Add flour a little bit at a time until mixture is firm and has the consistence of bread dough. Add nuts.

Shape into small disc shapes and bake at 325 degrees until edges are lightly browned. Cool on a cookie rack until room temperature. Sprinkle or roll in powdered sugar. Serve and enjoy.

The Hope Quilt

Susan Goggins

Grandma Goggins' Biscuits

DIRECTIONS:

Pour a five-pound bag of self-rising flour (maybe a little more) into a big bowl. Melt three heaping tablespoons of lard (Crisco will do) in a small skillet.

Hollow out a hole in the flour, but don't go all the way to the bottom of the bowl with it. Pour about three-quarters of the lard into the hole. Pour about a cup of buttermilk on top of the lard.

Rake a little of the flour around the edges of the hole into the hole on top of the liquid. Start swirling the mixture around and around and up and down, letting the liquid gather up the surrounding (and underneath) flour as you go. Slowly add another cup or more of buttermilk as you go.

When you get a good ball of dough, roll it out, cut your biscuits, and put them in a greased pan. Drizzle the remaining melted lard on top of the biscuits, and cook at 450 degrees until golden brown.

The Sun, the Moon, and a Box Of Divinity

Clara Wimberly

Divinity Candy

INGREDIENTS:

5 cups sugar
1 cup white Karo Syrup
1 cup water
Whites from 3 eggs
2 teaspoons vanilla
1/2 cup nuts

DIRECTIONS:

Cook sugar, syrup and water to soft-ball stage. Take out 1 cup and stir into stiffly beaten egg whites. Put remaining mixture back on fire, and cook to hard-ball stage. Pour slowly into egg mixture, beating continuously. Add vanilla and nuts; beat until it starts to harden. Pour into greased pan to cool. Cut into squares while still warm.

Mommy Darlin'

Debra Dixon

Saint Bubba's Chili

OK, there's always going to be that argument, beans or no beans? While I never listen to folks from Texas on the subject of barbecue (they think that beef is barbecue), they do know a thing or three about chili, and in the Terlingua International Chili Championship (the chili equivalent of the Memphis In May World Championship Barbecue competition), the rule is NO BEANS! That's good enough for me. If you want to add beans, feel free.

INGREDIENTS:

2-3 lbs. ground round (or you can used shredded chuck steak for a different texture)
2 cloves of garlic (finely chopped) per pound of meat
1 tablespoon extra virgin olive oil per pound of meat
2 10-ounce cans of Ro*Tel tomatoes
1 10-ounce can of tomato sauce
2 small jalapeno peppers, seeded and diced
1 teaspoon finely chopped fresh cilantro
1/2 cup chili powder
1 teaspoon cumin or 1 teaspoon finely chopped oregano
1 teaspoon sifted masa flour

DIRECTIONS:

Brown the meat in the olive oil in a large Dutch oven or stock pot. Drain, but not thoroughly. Add the remaining ingredients except the masa flour into the pot and then add water, just enough so that the liquid is almost level with the top of the ingredients in the pot and stir.

Bring to a boil, then cover and reduce to a simmer. Simmer over low heat for at least 2 hours, but 3 is better. Stir often. About 20 minutes before the chili is done, add the flour and stir in completely. Serve with chopped red onion and shredded cheddar or Monterey Jack cheese.

The Vinegar Files

Lynda Holmes

Vinegar Pie

INGREDIENTS:

1 stick margarine
2 teaspoons vinegar
1 cup sugar
1 teaspoon vanilla
2 eggs
2/3 cup chopped nuts
1 unbaked pie shell

DIRECTIONS:

Melt margarine; add sugar and eggs and beat together. Add vinegar, vanilla, and nuts. Pour into unbaked pie shell. Bake at 350 degrees for 30 minutes.

A Family Treasure

Susan Sipal

My Great-Grandma Leah was known for her sweet potato pudding. She always cooked it in a cast-iron skillet on her old wood stove for holidays and family gatherings (which was every Sunday). I like to carry on her tradition—minus the old wood stove.

Sweet Potato Pudding

INGREDIENTS:

4 cups grated raw sweet potatoes
2 eggs, un-separated, beaten
1 stick butter
1 cup sugar
1 tsp. vanilla
1/4 teaspoon allspice
1/4 teaspoon cinnamon
1/4 teaspoon nutmeg
1 teaspoon salt
2 tablespoons flour
Milk to make a soft batter (1and 1/2 cups probably)

DIRECTIONS:

Grate potatoes finely. In a bowl, mix well-beaten eggs, melted butter and sugar. Add potatoes and vanilla, spices, salt and flour. Stir until well mixed. Add milk to make a very soft batter, but not watery. Bake in oven at 350, stirring occasionally until it begins to thicken—about 1 hour. Then bake until top is brown and crusty.

This is so good, I usually like to double the recipe—if you've got a big enough skillet.

A Sunday Dress

Betty Cordell

Creamed Corn

INGREDIENTS:

8 ears sweet corn (Silver Queen or comparable)
Butter or margarine
Flour
Milk
Salt and pepper to taste

Directions:

Cut kernels off corn, cutting some in half, then scrape down to the cob, reserving the corn "milk"
Melt 2-4 tablespoons butter over medium heat
Add 1/4 cup flour to melted butter and stir in with a fork
Add milk gradually, stirring it in, until liquid is thick and smooth.
Add corn and corn "milk" gradually, stirring it in.
Simmer about 20 minutes, stirring to prevent milk from scorching.
Salt and pepper to taste.
Serves 6.

Note: My daddy, who was raised on a North Georgia farm, preferred his creamed corn cold and covered in pepper.

Barbie's Elopement
Sandra Chastain

Wedding Pound Cake

INGREDIENTS:
2 sticks of real butter, softened
3 cups of sugar
6 eggs
3 cups sifted self-rising flour
1 teaspoon vanilla
1/4 teaspoon baking soda
1 small size sour cream

DIRECTIONS:
Have ingredients at room temperature.
Cream butter and sugar.
Beat into mixture 2 eggs with 1 cup of flour until all is used.
Add soda to sour cream, then to mixture. Will be fluffy.
Add 1 teaspoon vanilla.
Bake in LARGE tube or bundt pan for 1 hour and 20 minutes at 300 degrees.

This is my pound cake recipe. It can be made in two makings for a small wedding cake.

FROM DEBORAH SMITH: The Mermaid of Cow Pie Spring

A mermaid never lets herself sink to the bottom.
—Patsy McGee

Patsy McGee was just 20 years old when she fled along the back roads of northern Florida on that fateful summer night in 1950, a green-eyed, sunburned head-turner with a lustrous swoop of auburn hair and a thick cracker drawl straight out of the dirt-poor fishing camps and watermelon farms far from the tourist beaches. She'd given birth down in Tampa only that morning. It felt as if someone had pushed a bowling ball out of her body, and her breasts ached with milk. Even her wedding band hurt as it lay heavy on her chest by a thin gold chain, hidden. Her newborn son, Paul, slept beside her in a half-bushel tomato basket on the black cloth seat of Patsy's old Studebaker sedan.

Upon leaving Tampa, Patsy had hurriedly swaddled the baby in the makeshift bassinet, lining the basket with a pink blanket on which she'd embroidered mermaids, daisies, and several fish that might be whales or might be largemouth bass. Tasteful art was not Patsy's forte. Hidden in the Studebaker's trunk were several costumes Patsy had stolen when Weeki

Wachee Springs, near St. Petersburg, had fired her from their mermaid show. Beneath the beautiful mermaid tails lay a small blue suitcase crusted with dried mud and sand. Inside the suitcase was twenty thousand dollars in small bills. Patsy had carefully wrapped the packets in aluminum foil before burying them inside the suitcase. She didn't trust banks. She had grown up on the fading cusp of the Depression, listening to her granny curse them.

Patsy was nothing if not sincere in her beliefs, right or wrong. The first red-headed Scottish McGee had sunk his shabby boots into the muck of a Florida shore in the 1700's. Ever since, generations of McGee's had made their staunchly ordinary Southern livings—farming, fishing, and drinking—in the sub-tropical pine forests and sandy small towns of the state's panhandle, that less-celebrated top half of Florida where a fall frost actually colors the trees and dulls the oleander shrubs.

But Patsy was special. She was a mermaid.

She had known so since childhood. A mother can run away, a father can die, and a grandma with nothing but a fish camp cabin for a home can raise an abandoned child with no more love than she'd give a stray puppy, but if that child finds a dream to hold onto, she'll survive. Patsy had found her dream early on, in the water.

She'd grown up swimming fearlessly in the depths of a pond-sized puddle named Coohatchee Springs, on the Florida-Alabama border near Tallahassee, where Granny McGee worked as a cook for well-to-do businessmen who came from as far away as Jacksonville to rough it in cabins stocked with bourbon and cigars while casting their lines for giant catfish and bass.

Coohatchee Springs. In Creek Indian, the word *hatchee* meant water, river, stream. But nobody could say for sure where the *coo* in *Coohatchee* came from, so as a child, Patsy credited the name to the spring's population of soft gray doves. *Coo Hatchee*. Dove Water. Patsy liked that image. Everybody said the doves were just ordinary birds, but the doves didn't agree. They cooed and strutted happily among the far showier herons and egrets and kingfishers on the spring's dock. Like Patsy, they refused to be ignored. The tiny spring was blue, like turquoise sky; to Patsy, swimming in it was like flying, like being a bird, escaping from the heat, the mosquitoes, the loneliness. Patsy searched for something that only seemed to exist in a fluid state, and she found it in the water.

"Little lady, did you know you're swimming in the tiptop of a fluid world so deep it might come out on the other end off the coast of China?" a visiting fisherman had asked Patsy once. The man said he studied the ways of water for the government, so Patsy figured he knew what he was talking about.

"All the way to China?" she'd breathed, transfixed. The old folks like to say if you dug a hole deep enough, you might go all the way through to the bottom of the world and hit China. "Is it true?"

"Yes, indeed. A spring's not the same as a lake, you know. A lake's just a puddle on the surface of the earth; it gets its water from the top—from rain, from the creeks that feed it, from run-off. But a spring, ah! A spring gets its water straight from the heart of the planet. Spring water bubbles up through cracks and caves in the limestone bedrock. This whole part of northern Florida is sitting on that bedrock, as if planted on top of a flat rock sponge or a slab of Swiss cheese. There's water trickling beneath every step we take, water slipping up and over and down and in and out through wondrous tunnels and caverns until it finds an open bowl in the limestone right up at the top, like this little spring, in the sunshine. And so that, little lady, is what Coohatchee Springs is. A bottomless limestone bowl."

"Bottomless?" She had clasped her hands to her heart, trying to imagine. She was only ten at the time; infinity was a million years.

"Yes, bottomless, indeed. Because somewhere way down in the deepest, coldest pit of this spring you'll find the spring's pipes. Where the water squeezes up through layer upon layer of limestone."

"If I dived down to the bottom, I could swim inside one of those pipes?"

"No, now, little lady, even this tiny fishing puddle of a spring is too deep for you to do that. I'm sure its pipes—those limestone caves and tunnels full of aquifer water that feed it—are too narrow for even a little girl to squeeze into. But just you picture it! Endless roots of water, stretching from this very place you swim down through the limestone, down and down and down—"

"All the way to China!"

The man laughed and nodded. "All the way to the other side of the world."

Patsy never forgot his description. He confirmed what she felt, that she belonged to a magical realm of bottomless springs atop a hidden realm of moving water, connected to exotic and distant lands.

"Nothin' but a bunch of hooey," Granny McGee drawled at such ideas. She knew her place in life, and it wasn't fancy. She cleaned and packed the fishermen's catches in metal coolers of ice for the trip back to the city, or she'd cook up the fish for the men to gobble down right there at the camp's picnic tables. Granny McGee floated forever in Patsy's mind, a stout old manatee of a woman, grim and tough, always sweating in a straw hat and baggy overalls, her thick, reddened hands dropping cornmeal battered fish into huge cast iron skillets bubbling full of melted lard over a coal cook stove. Her kitchen had been a screened porch overlooking the lake.

When Patsy swam as a child, she often lifted her head from the water to catch the scent of the open-air skillets. To her, the aroma was her grandmother's way of calling her home, a sign of love that needed no words, some slim proof that Patsy might be wanted. Granny McGee only gave her one gift in all those years. When Patsy was about twelve, the old lady bought her a book from a peddler.

The Little Mermaid, by Hans Christian Andersen. Patsy read it until the pages fell apart, then glued them back together and read them some more. The tragedy, oh! The beauty of the little mermaid's courage when she traded her fins for legs, the heartbreaking unfairness and betrayal when her prince fell in love with an ordinary mortal! The story wasn't so much a fairytale as an anthem for unsentimental inspiration.

Don't ever give up lovin' the water, Patsy decided. *It's the only thing that'll always love you back. The only thing that's bottomless.*

She promised herself she wouldn't end up moping for a prince who didn't appreciate her, that she'd never give up her fins for ordinary legs. Mermaids were destined for greatness, even given their darkest tribulations on dry land.

Life had seemed so easy to predict, then.

Light-headed and in pain, Patsy swigged a bottle of tepid Coca-Cola with four aspirins and two packets of BC Headache Powder in it, trying to dull the pain between her legs as she drove. Sweat dappled her plaid blouse and pink peddle-pushers. Moths and bats darted in front of the car. With the window down to catch the breeze, she worried that they might zoom inside.

"Get away, you wild things, I got a new baby in here," she yelled, then downshifted the Studebaker and blew the horn. A startled deer bounded across the road and disappeared into the pines like a shadow. Somewhere in the forest, a wildcat screamed.

She slowed as the road narrowed to cross a rattling, one-lane wooden bridge. Lost and exhausted, she squinted through the narrow tunnel of light the dusty Studebaker's headlights made on pale macadam flecked with crushed oyster shells. Pitch-black forest and pine swamp crowded the road on both sides; there wasn't a streetlight or house light to be seen in any direction. Frogs sang loud enough to drown out a hellfire preacher yelling about Communists on the radio, and the occasional low grunt of an alligator sounded from the woods.

U.S. 1, the old federal two-lane that funneled wood-paneled deluxe station wagons full of tourist families down the East Coast to Florida's Atlantic beaches, was less than an hour's drive east of Patsy that night. If she aimed the Studebaker due west, she could make Panama City, on the Gulf, by dawn. The state's northern coasts were still mostly wild places of beautiful dunes and shifting sea oats, speckled with pastel motor courts and diners, reptile exhibits and parrot shows. There were no interstates, no super highways, no cookie-cutter hotel chains, no Disney.

Instead, there were tiny motels shaped like teepees or igloos or any other thing the imagination could fathom, and restaurants shaped like pirate ships or castles, and candy shops tucked inside fake plaster volcanoes, and real alligators swimming decoratively along the blue concrete creeks of fake jungle gardens. Florida was the land of daydreams and entrepreneurial whimsy. Along the slow, sunny routes to the beach, colorful nonsense lured visitors and their money. Among all those oddball wonders of the world, Weeki Wachee Springs with its mermaid show was, in Patsy's opinion, the pinnacle of true class.

But on that night, Patsy only trusted the wild, quiet backbone of her state, far from the tourist lights. Her home territory, where the crystal clear waters of ancient aquifers percolated up through the sand and rock to form springs so magical that swimming in them was like visiting the underwater castle of a princess. She needed a dose of that homegrown fantasy again. She needed a plate of black-eyed peas, corn fritters, and fried trout; she needed to swing slowly in a front porch hammock; she needed a backwoods tent preacher to lay his palm on her head and pronounce her healed without a shred of doubt; she needed refuge.

Patsy pawed at the radio dial. *Screech, scratch, squawk.* Saturday night preachers, baseball games, the Grand Ol' Opry, and rock n' roll. Finally, the tuner struck gold.

I don't care if the sun don't shine, Patti Page sang. Patti was one of Patsy's inspirations, not just because they shared a similar first name, but because Patti Page had suffered for her art, like Patsy. Patti Page had been born barefoot and dirt-poor in Oklahoma, but was now so rich and famous she even had a title, like some kind of queen. *Patti Page, the Singing Rage.* Yet Patsy couldn't bear listening to her newest song, *The Tennessee Waltz.* It was too heartbreaking. All that lost love.

Patsy mulled her tongue in a dry mouth. She glanced nervously in the Studebaker's rearview mirror.

"I guess if anybody cared enough to chase me they'd have chased me by now," she said aloud. Patsy clutched the steering wheel hard with her sweaty left hand and fumbled across the seat with her right one, gently coming to rest on Paul's velvet-skinned forehead. "You just ignore these noises and keep on sleepin', honey, 'cause I'm not gonna let nothin' or nobody get the best of us again. And nobody's ever takin' you away from me." The green glow of the dashboard lights gave the newborn an aquamarine tint, as if he were floating underwater. "You're the son of a mermaid," Patsy whispered. "I'll find us some water to live by."

The first time Patsy swam at Weeki Wachee, during auditions for the mermaid show, she looked down happily at the soft, mysterious, turbulent darkness far below. *I can almost see China from here*, she thought.

In terms of waterpower, Weeki Wachee dwarfed the Coohatchee. Its sparkling depths filled a craggy limestone pool as big as a football field. During the war, Navy divers in heavy suits and helmets had explored more than a hundred feet down, but still found no bottom. They were nearly bowled over by currents spewing up from vents in the rocks. They reported that the spring rose out of grand underwater caves tall enough to stand in. Who knew how far those fabulous and mysterious roots might reach?

Patsy loved everything about working at Weeki Wachee. It was no mean feat to be selected as one of the twenty girls in the legendary swimming troupe. A mermaid had to be able to hold her breath for at least two minutes while smiling, swimming in choreographed synch with the other girls, miming the words to a song, changing costumes behind a rock, and even pretending to eat or drink, a bit of razzle-dazzle that always brought wild applause from the audience.

A mermaid had not only to be pretty, athletic, and graceful, but also brave enough not to panic when small alligators occasionally joined the show. After all, the show's auditorium was part of the spring's open basin. The theater's pastel wooden structure curved along one shore. Audiences walked down steps to tiers of seats sixteen feet beneath the spring's surface, where a long glass wall made a window into the spring's beautiful water, glowing with pastel lights.

"This place's like a huge fish tank, and we're the fish on display," one girl said with a shudder during the auditions. "I bet some folks tap on the glass just to see if we'll hide like trout."

"I'll never hide," Patsy told her. "I'm not a trout. I'm a princess of the water, and people are meant to admire me."

Indeed, at Weeki Wachee, she became a star. The audience loved her. People wanted to pose for pictures with her; children wanted her autograph, and cute college boys from the University of Florida, over in Gainesville, asked her out on dates, which was against Weeki Wachee policy. She'd obeyed the rules proudly and had dreamed of a long future in the bright lights beneath the water. She'd even worked as an extra in a Hollywood movie filmed at the springs. *Mr. Peabody and the Mermaid,* starring William Powell. Her scene had been cut from the final movie, but still. There she was, immortalized on film, at least in spirit.

"I'm a mermaid and a movie actress," she had taken to telling people.

And a good mermaid virgin. Truly. Unlike *The Little Mermaid,* Patsy waited wisely for a prince who wouldn't ask her to sacrifice her fins.

One day, she found him. Or thought she had.

Paul Hampenstein, the fourth, of the Massachusetts Hampensteins, came to Florida for the same reason as every other red-blooded college student. Spring Break. Weeki Wachee Springs was supposed to be just a quick laugh stop for him and his fraternity buddies, who were headed to the Gulf beaches after two days of non-stop driving. All they really wanted were some wholesome Weeki Wachee postcards to send Mumsie and Dads as evidence that Spring Break was about something other than beer and sex.

For Patsy, posing in full fin for visitors and their boxy little Kodaks was usually a great part of the job. She smiled as old men kissed her cheek and teenage boys gawked in blushing arousal; she was super-nice to the women and teenage girls so they wouldn't think she was a tramp, or stuck-up. She doted on the children, who gazed at her in utter wonder.

"Every girl is a mermaid at heart," she'd tell them, "and every boy has to earn the right to a mermaid's love. Being a mermaid means a girl is true and strong and trustworthy. Like being a Scout, only with flippers."

But the college boys were just there to leer and laugh. They showed no respect. *Hey gorgeous, what's hidden in your tail? Is your lipstick waterproof? Let me test it.*

Paul had walked up in the midst of his pals saying such things to Patsy. He frowned, then turned to them and said in his stern important-sounding Massachusetts accent, "That'll be enough, you apes."

The jerks shrugged and laughed and wandered off as if they owned the sunshine in their polished loafers and fancy slacks and golf shirts. Patsy's rescuer smiled at her. "I apologize. You must put up with a lot of junk from ignorant people. Personally, I think you're the only girl I've ever met who looks perfectly happy to be who she is." Patsy stared at him in hypnotized silence. She felt as if she were floating in ethereal water instead of perched on a blue-painted granite rock by a *Take Your Picture with a Weeki Wachee Mermaid* sign. She had never been speechless before in her entire life, yet there she was, deprived of a tongue like a demon-strangled woman she'd seen once at a Pentecostal tent revival near Palatka.

"You're the smartest boy I've ever met," she finally managed.

He smiled wider. "May I sit down? Will you tell me what it's like to be a mermaid?"

"You bet!"

He sat beside her on the rock without a shred of embarrassment, and she began to talk to him. And he listened. He really listened. He was special. She knew that from the first moment. An aura of quiet confidence radiated from him. He held her gaze without dropping his eyes to her heavily pleated bra, even once. At least not when she noticed, which was fine. He was tall and lean and handsomely long-faced, with big, sweet, dark-blue eyes and a broad smile.

Eventually he mentioned that his father was a business partner of somebody named Joe Kennedy, up in Massachusetts; that meant nothing to Patsy, except that Paul mentioned playing touch football at Hyannis Port with a Kennedy son who planned to run for U.S. Senate.

"So?" she'd said, flustered. "Running for something and gettin' it are two different things."

"You're just not impressed by much, are you?" Paul answered, laughing. "Not impressed by money and college boys from Yankee states, for sure."

"Nope. Because I know who I am, I'm an aqua-theatrical actress," she replied with utter seriousness. "I uphold a tradition of mermaid womanhood that is smart and classy and choosy. I grew up in a fish camp knowing how to catch brim, and bait a crawdad trap, and make hush puppies out of coarse corn meal and lard and a little sugar. I won't ever go hungry. I know who I am, and I'm a mermaid. So I don't need to be impressed by much." She paused, feeling her face turn hot, her eyes wanting to be shy. "But I am impressed by you. Because you know who you are, too."

"I'm the guy who's going to marry you," he answered.

After another speechless moment, she agreed that he was right.

Two days later they drove east all the way to the Atlantic coast. Near Daytona they honeymooned at a tiny blue concrete motel cabin with a rattling window fan. Sand sifted under the door, and the cypress plank walls smelled like turpentine. Once, when Patsy threw back her hands in ecstasy, she scraped her knuckles on the periwinkle shells glued to the bed's pine headboard in the shape of palm tree.

Paul died the next weekend, as he drove back to college. His friends weren't with him; they'd gone their own way after he scolded them that first day at Weeki Wachee. At home they told their parents and friends about the gold-digging hick who'd snared Paul in a quickie marriage.

Patsy didn't have much time to mourn the husband she'd only known for a week. Paul's family sent a lawyer, the suitcase full of money, and a threat. In a rare moment of fear and confusion, Patsy took the money, buried it, and promised never to tell a soul about the marriage.

A couple of months later, when she realized she was pregnant, she tried to hide the fact and keep performing at Weeki Wachee. It was easy at first; Patsy's tummy bulge only gave her a more voluptuous look. She sewed panels into the girdle-like tops of the mermaid tails so they'd expand around her growing waist, and secretly let out the straps of her costume tops to accommodate her fattening breasts.

She fantasized about giving birth in secret then hiring some nice, country woman, colored or white, to watch the baby during the day and going back to work as a Weeki Wachee mermaid, as if nothing had changed.

But when Patsy was six months along the costume manager caught wise, and Patsy's mermaid career cruised to a dead stop. Weeki Wachee's rules of conduct couldn't be breeched: Only unmarried girls could be mermaids. Unmarried, untouched, wholesome virgins. Period.

Devastated, Patsy retreated to a boarding house across the bay in Tampa. She told the old lady who owned the boarding house that her husband was away in the Navy, then took a job as a Woolsworth clerk while she waited for the baby to come. She intended to give birth alone in her rented room; she didn't want to answer any tricky questions at the Tampa hospital. Why get doctors involved in something Mother Nature intended to be, well, natural? After all, she herself had been born in a pine-board cabin at the fish camp, and she had turned out just fine.

Patsy didn't count on going into labor two weeks early, while standing behind the Maybelline counter. She watched in horrified fascination as fluid stained her pink maternity skirt and dribbled in small rivers down her nylons, finally making puddles in her white pumps. The next thing she knew, she lay flat on her back on the linoleum floor, clutching her belly, and someone had called an ambulance.

The next morning, after hours of groaning labor followed by the drugged nothingness of a modern 1950's hospital delivery, Patsy looked up groggily into the beady, bespectacled eyes of a white-capped nurse. The nurse stared at her over a clipboard.

"I'm fillin' out a birth certificate for your girl. Name of the baby's daddy?"

Patsy tried to focus, but the recovery room kept shifting. Suddenly it faded away, opening like a melted curtain, and there stood Paul stood, tall and sweet-homely and wonderful, smiling at her with the ocean and sky and beach behind him. Just like he had when he was alive, on their honeymoon. She would love him all her life. He had respected her dreams. He had believed in mermaids.

"Dead," she said brokenly. Warnings curled through her mind like alligators, but she couldn't catch one by the tail long enough to heed it. "Dead." Patsy felt like crying, but the alligators scared her out of it. Mermaids couldn't cry around alligators. You had to show them who was the boss of the water.

"Dead, where?"

"In his. . .Cor. . .vette."

The nurse leaned closer. "Where?" Patsy gagged at a whiff of starchy powder.

"On the highway between. . .here and. . .his school up north. . .called Harvard. You. . .go. . .away, now. You. . .smell. . .dried out. . .to me."

The nurse hunched over her. She spoke in a voice that could crack the shell on a snapping turtle. "Look here, Little Miss Wise-Acre, *where is your husband?*"

"Up. . .north."

"Where?"

"Where dead people go when they're angels. I know. . .he's there. He's in Heaven."

"*Where* is he buried?"

"Dead is dead. Wherever they bury you, that's. . .where you are."

A vein throbbed in the nurse's forehead. "You got a marriage license?"

"Not. . .anymore."

"Why?"

"He had it. . .with him. It burned up."

"Burned up?"

Patsy moaned. "In the car wreck."

"Your husband burned up in a car wreck on the highway between here and somewhere? When?"

"Last. . .summer."

"Then how'd you get in the family way?"

"I didn't know I was. . .in the way. Family way. When he. . .when he died. He didn't know. We didn't know. We met when he was spring break. It hadn't been long."

"Uh huh. I see. Where'd y'all get married? What county? What town?"

"Daytona Beach. Justice of the. . .peace."

"Then there'll be a certificate on file."

"No. Not anymore."

"Beg pardon?"

"His family. . .they got rid of it. Got rid of me, too. Told me to. . .go away."

"Uh huh." The nurse stared into Patsy's eyes. Patsy tried to stare back but could only make out a pair of blurry, mean eyeballs framed by the twin wings of black reading glasses. The nurse snorted. "You better come up with a better story than that, or I'm callin' the county welfare office to come see whether you're really married. Whether you're fit to raise a child."

Patsy panicked. The alligators were breathing right in her face. They had bad teeth and chewed peppermint gum to hide the stink. "Paul," she said brokenly.

The nurse scowled. "That your husband? Paul? Paul who?"

"Paul . . . Hampenstein."

"Hampen *what*?"

"Stein."

"Tine? Like a tine on a fork?"

Patsy maneuvered her tongue slowly and spelled *stein*. "Paul. Crispin. Hampenstein. The fourth."

The nurse straightened with a huff. She scribbled heavily on her clipboard. "What kinda name is that?"

"A *rich* one."

"Huh." The nurse shoved her pencil behind one ear and turned to leave. Patsy wobbled upright in bed, swaying. "Where's my baby?"

"She's being fed in the nursery. You'll get to hold her when you're more awake."

"I want to see her *now*. I'll feed her. You bring her." Patsy waved in the direction of her breasts. "I've got milk. Gallons of it, feels like."

The nurse rolled her eyes. "This is a modern hospital. Only animals feed their young that way. Only white trash."

White trash. Fightin' words to a fish camp girl. Patsy straightened slowly. "I'm a mermaid. Mermaids know what. . .what titties are for. You're so damn dumb you don't even know. . .that you got a pair."

The insult hit the nurse right between the eyes and trailed down her face like spit off a hard rock. Her crow-winged eyes narrowed to slivers. "White trash," she repeated. "Dead rich Yankee husband, my hind foot. Harvard. Hampenstein. We'll just see about all *that*. If you got in-laws, they'll want to know about their grandbaby."

The nurse stomped out.

Patsy pushed herself out of bed. Her legs collapsed. She sat down hard, spreading her hands on the cold tile floor, searching for something to hold onto. Paul's people had shoved money at her, had told her to get lost and never use his name as her own, but what if they found out he had a son? Would they want the baby? Would they try to take him?

Patsy swore softly. "I'm not givin' up anybody else I love."

She crawled to her purse and overnight case, perched atop

a metal dresser. It seemed to take hours but she finally managed to pull on a plaid blouse, pink peddle-pushers, and penny loafers. Patsy staggered down the hall to the nursery. A dozen babies were asleep in their bassinets, and all the nurses were busy elsewhere. Holding onto an empty incubator for support, Patsy rolled straight to a tiny baby boy with a pale fluff of red hair. She knew it was her baby before she lifted the tag on the bassinet.

Baby McGee, Boy, the tag read.

Nurse No-Titties hadn't had a chance to correct the last name, yet. Hadn't had a chance to call any rich, mean Hampensteins, yet. Patsy carefully lifted the baby into her arms. "Time to head for warmer water, sweetie," she whispered. "This is a cold, dry world you've been born into."

Patsy toted her son out a back door, weaving as gracefully as a tired angel fish under the hot Florida sun.

"I will not sink to the bottom," Patsy shouted as she drove, half-fainting, through the night.

Paul uttered a soft, smacking sound then yawned without opening her eyes. Patsy looked at him anxiously. His head was shaped like a mashed orange and his complexion had the pink, vein-speckled appearance of boiled shrimp. But he was the most beautiful sight Patsy had ever seen.

"I'm prayin' for us, honey," Patsy whispered. "Granny McGee always said I got no common sense. But who wants to have something that's 'common?' Just low and ordinary and boring—is that what common sense is? Just makin' do with the mud hole God stuck you in? If God didn't want me to meet your daddy, then how come I did? If God didn't want me to be a mermaid, then how come God gave me the dream? If God didn't want me to have you, how come you're here?

No, baby boy, God didn't set me up to take a dive. I know the world is low and mean and common and dry as a bone, but I intend to swim for glory, anyhow." She hesitated, fighting tears. "But God better hurry up and give me a sign that we're not up a creek without a paddle."

Patsy guided the Studebaker around a wooded curve. An odd pink light winked at her through the pines ahead. She leaned forward, squinting. A light in the darkness.

The woods opened up a little. A dirt lane curled off to the right beside a white mailbox on a leaning wooden post. Beneath a pink light bulb covered by a rusting tin shade hung a pink metal sign in the shape of a cow. The cow's tail pointed down the lane.

Cow Pie Springs Motor Court And Diner.

Air Conditioned Rooms

Fresh Ice

Home Cooking

See The Most Beautiful Spring In These Parts

Patsy sucked in a long breath. A motel with a spring. Wonderful! Even if it *was* named for cow manure.

She downshifted and woozily stuck out one hand to signal the turn for any phantom cars. Slowly she swung the Studebaker down the lane beside the pointing cow. Steadying Paul's tomato-basket bassinet with one hand, Patsy clutched the car's steering wheel as it bounced and bumped. Pines leaned inward over the lane, curious and watching. Yet the road was prettily lined by daisies amidst the sharp fans of palmetto shrubs.

After about a minute the woods opened up. A dimly lit oasis of pink stucco cottages rose like an island from the earthy loneliness of soft, sweaty forest. To one side sat a little pink cottage with a pink-lighted OFFICE sign in the window. Huge oaks trailed Spanish moss above a graveled parking lot lined with big rocks painted pink with white tops like craggy nipples. Other than an ancient red truck parked beside the cottage, there were no other vehicles in sight. The Cow Pie Springs Motor Court wasn't exactly a hotspot on the east-west tourist route.

Patsy didn't care. Her eyes were riveted to the silver gleam of a large pond beyond the parking lot. A ramshackle picket fence surrounded it, tilting and wandering, a carefree whitewashed ribbon following the soft, grassy shore with no serious intent to keep cows or any other creature from reaching the water. An oak dipped one gnarled arm into the pond, the bend of the oak's elbow forming a natural bench out over the water.

"It's beautiful. It's magic," Patsy whispered.

Cow Pie Spring. It was no Weeki Wachee—maybe only half that size, meaning any football game played on its surface would start at one goalpost and end at the fifty-yard line. A pretty creek flowed from the spring and ran beneath the road before disappearing into the forest. Patsy, barely breathing, eased the Studebaker over a narrow bridge made of coquina stone, as if carved from pale coral. Like driving over a tiny reef that separated the outside world from the watery kingdom of the Cow Pies.

"Oh honey, oh sweetie," she crooned to the spring and her baby. She pulled Paul's tomato basket closer. "Come to Mama."

Patsy parked the car with its headlights turned on the spring. Carrying Paul, she stumbled to the ribbon of knee-high picket fence, clambered over it, kicked off her loafers, then sank down on the muddy shore and thrust her bare feet so deep into the water it soaked the calf-high hems of her peddle pushers.

"Revival," she moaned.

She laid the yawning baby on her thighs. Moaning and rocking, Patsy scooped a hand into the spring. "I'm gonna christen us. First, me." Patsy splashed water on her face. "I'm Patsy Darlene McGee Hampenstein. Even if I can *never* tell anybody. I'll never forget." Crying just a little, Patsy scooped up another handful of water, let most of it dribble through her fingers, then gently smoothed the moisture on their son's forehead, cheeks, and lips.

"I christen you Paul Patrick Hampenstein, the *fifth*. But I can't ever tell you that. You'll just have to be happy bein' plain Paul McGee. We gotta be what we're meant to be, sweetie, and a name's just a name. I can't let the Hampensteins find you. I'm so sorry I can't ever tell you I named you after your daddy. Paul. And Patrick, after *me*. Sort of. Patsy. Patrick. It's as close as I can get."

Paul Patrick Hampenstein the fifth yawned and gurgled, unimpressed. Patsy leaned back, eyes shut, letting the spring wash away her fear, worry, humiliation. Head up, she sighed a long breath of release, then opened her eyes. The Studebaker's high beams cast a misty spotlight all the way to the spring's far edge. There, near the grand oak with its arm bent over the water, stood a big, bright, hand-painted sign.

FOR SALE
THIS MOTOR COURT AND OWNER'S HOUSE
ON 52 ACRES
INCLUDING THIS PRETTY SPRING
— NONE OTHER LIKE IT!
ALL YOURS, FOR ONLY $6,000

Patsy's mouth opened in a silent gape of awe, a voiceless, mermaid-underwater prayer of homecoming and gratitude.

"Girl, are you and your youngun' okay?" a gnarled old-man voice twanged behind her. "Y'all cain't sit here at night. We got gators that might getcha."

"Leave her be, old man," an equally gnarled old-woman voice scolded. "Cain't you see she needs to sit in the spring more'n she needs to worry about a couple of piddly gators?"

Hypnotized by fate, Patsy twisted slowly. As if in a dream she looked up into a pair of kind, sunburned faces. Backwoods folks. Her sort of people. The sort of folks who understood the love of hidden water. The spring's guardian angels. And hers.

Finally she came up for air.

"I'm the mermaid of Cow Pie Springs," she told them calmly. "I'm goin' to buy this place and make it famous."

And she did.

Acknowledgements

Fly By Night is dedicated to the memory of my Great Aunt Charlotte, on whom the character Sophie is based. When you're young, there's always one person in your life who is simply...magic to you. She was mine. And, Dad, thank you for giving me this crazy blessing called writing. Or, maybe it's a curse. Either way, it's all your fault. —Sarah Addison Allen

Hair Today, Gone Tomorrow To my daughter Cynthia, to my husband, patron, and muse Wes, and to Big Mama, who loves me like I was her own. —Maureen Hardegree

The Fan Dancer In memory of my mother, who inspired this story—albeit unintentionally. —Bert Goolsby

The Healing Touch This story is dedicated to Deborah Smith, for her kindness and interest in a new writer. Warm thanks to Jill Jones, a true friend and writing companion. Last, but not least, to my finest teacher at UNC-Chapel Hill, Doris Betts. I am truly, after two decades and a few years, your late bloomer. —Susan Alvis

The Hope Quilt Thank you to my beloved grandparents: Elmer and Gladys Hardy, and Pink and Winnie Goggins; and to my adored great-grandmother, Jewell Hendrick—at whose knees I heard the tales my own stories spring from. —Susan Goggins

The Sun, the Moon, and a Box Of Divinity I hope this story will give my family an insight into the sweet, simple life, as it was when I was a girl. Especially my grandchildren: Hannah, Lindsey, Lucas and Emory. I love you all very much. —Clara Wimberly

Dirty Harry, the Mule To my wife Lisa and daughters Jennifer and Megan: All my love—and my thanks for putting up with the time I spend writing. And to Susan Goggins and Susan "Smokey" Trudeau: Thanks for all your help, encouragement and critiques. —Mike Roberts

Mommy Darlin' For Bill Dixon—the best kid ever and a darned fine man. —Debra Dixon

The Vinegar Files Thank you to my entire family, whose constant love, support, and memories fuel my desire to write. Thank you to the Lord, who has led me to share my faith with others through writing. —Lynda Holmes

A Family Treasure For my family—Daddy, Mama, Sharon, and Bill—I am, and have always been, truly blessed. —Susan Sipal

A Sunday Dress For Estelle Kyler who worked for my family as cook and housekeeper, as well as a child care giver, for 50 years. She was the best, most instinctive cook of Southern food I've ever known. —Betty Cordell

The Mermaid Of Cow Pie Spring As always, all my thanks and love to my very patient husband, Hank. —Deborah Smith

Order your copy of

SWEET TEA & JESUS SHOES

Book 1 in BelleBooks' Sweet Tea series

0-9673035-0-8 • $14.95

Come sit on the porch a spell. Let's talk about times gone by and folks we remember, about slow summer evenings and lightning bugs in a jar. Listen to the sound of a creaky swing and cicadas chorusing in the background. Let's talk about how things used to be in the South and, for some of us, the way they still are.

"The warm tones in this compilation of anecdotal reminiscences and personal essays beckon readers to pull up a chair and listen to tales of life in the South. Told with humor and honesty from the perspective of traditional and not-so-typical Southern Belles, the stories piece together a literary quilt of eccentricities in Southern living. The authors share their voices, memories, family secrets and personal disappointments. From tales of the familial tension between Smith's cleverly named "Mamaside" and "Daddyside," to Dixon's yarn about an aunt so mean her stare could "peel paint off the sides of completely weathered barns," the stories are creative and observant. Readers looking for proof that every family is just as off-kilter as their own will particularly enjoy this read. It's about living and loving and learning, regardless of which time zone you call home."
—*Today's Librarian*

Order your copy of

ALL GOD'S CREATURES

0-9673035-8-3 • $14.95

Say hello to Maggie McLain, an unlikely Southern debutante in 1960s Memphis. Gawky, restless, smart and opinionated, young Maggie isn't cut out to fill the patent leather pumps of a Southern belle. When she ditches a Cotton Carnival ball to save a drowning pup, Maggie realizes her destiny.

Is the land of mint juleps and Elvis ready for a woman veterinarian? Maybe not, but Dr. Maggie McLain sets out to prove otherwise.

Over the years, Maggie earns the devotion and respect of crusty farmers, snobby horse breeders and doubtful pet owners throughout western Tennessee. She's an inspiration to up-and-coming women vets, a loving wife to her proud husband, a patient mother to her demanding kids, and above all, a champion to sick and injured animals.

When loss and grief knock Maggie off her pedestal, she falls hard. It may take a miracle for her to understand that sometimes even the best doctor must struggle to heal her own heart.

"Steel Magnolias meets James Herriot. A warm and wonderful story of Southern veterinarians. I loved it."
—Patricia Potter, USA Today bestselling author

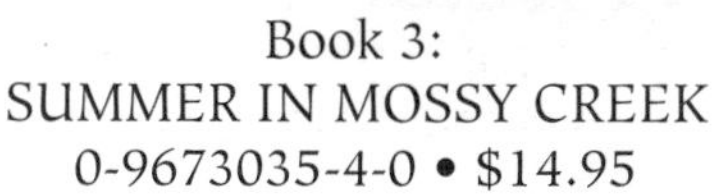
Book 3:
SUMMER IN MOSSY CREEK
0-9673035-4-0 • $14.95

Book 4:
BLESSINGS OF MOSSY CREEK
0-9673035-5-9 • $14.95

COMING in Fall 2005:
A Day In Mossy Creek, book five in the series

"MOSSY CREEK is as much fun as a cousin reunion; like sipping ice cold lemonade on a hot summer's afternoon. Hire me a moving van, it's the kind of town where everyone wishes they could live."*—Debbie Macomber, NYT Bestselling author*

"Mitford meets Mayberry in the first book of this innovative and warmhearted new series from BelleBooks, publisher of last year's award-winning southern anthology, ŒSweet Tea and Jesus Shoes." *—The Cleveland Daily Banner, Cleveland, Tennessee*

"I don't usually subscribe to the notion that it "takes a village to raise a child," but when the village is Mossy Creek, well I say more power to it. And any child raised here has surely been blessed by God." *—Jackie Cooper, WMAC-AM, Macon, Georgia*

The Mossy Creek Hometown Series

Available in all fine bookstores and direct from BelleBooks

Mossy Creek

Reunion at Mossy Creek

Summer in Mossy Creek

Blessings of Mossy Creek

Coming in Fall 2005

A Day in Mossy Creek

Other BelleBooks Titles

All God's Creatures
by Carolyn McSparren

BOOK ONE IN THE ***EVERYONE'S SPECIAL*** CHILDREN'S SERIES
by Sandra Chastain

KaseyBelle: The Tiniest Fairy in the Kingdom

Sweet Tea and Jesus Shoes
More Sweet Tea

THE WATERLILIES SERIES
by bestselling author Deborah Smith

Alice at Heart
Diary of a Radical Mermaid